CROSSHAIRS

Also by Harry Hunsicker

Still River
The Next Time You Die

CROSSHAIRS

HARRY HUNSICKER

THOMAS DUNNE BOOKS
ST. MARTIN'S MINOTAUR
NEW YORK

This is a work of fiction. All of the characters, organizations, and events portrayed in this novel are either products of the author's imagination or are used fictitiously.

THOMAS DUNNE BOOKS.
An imprint of St. Martin's Press.

www.thomasdunnebooks.com
www.minotaurbooks.com

Library of Congress Cataloging-in-Publication Data

Hunsicker, Harry.
    Crosshairs : a Lee Henry Oswald mystery / Harry Hunsicker.—1st ed.
        p.   cm.
    ISBN-13: 978-0-312-34851-9
    ISBN-10: 0-312-34851-7
  1. Private investigators—Texas—Dallas—Fiction. 2. Dallas (Tex.)—Fiction.
  I. Title.
    PS3608.U566C76   2007
    813'.6—dc22

                          2007013773

First Edition: August 2007

10 9 8 7 6 5 4 3 2 1

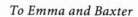

To Emma and Baxter

Acknowledgments

Bringing a book to life is a group effort. To that end I would like to thank Erin Brown, Sean Desmond, and everyone at St. Martin's Press, Minotaur, and Thomas Dunne Books for their dedication and professionalism. Also, a note of gratitude to Richard Abate for putting all the pieces together.

I would also like to thank Erika Barr, Jan Blankenship, Amy Bourret, Victoria Calder, Rita Chapman, Will Clarke, Paul Coggins, Fanchon Knott, Clif Nixon, David Norman, Brooke Malouf, and Max Wright for all their help and support. Special thanks to Amy Bourret, Suzanne Frank, and Dan Hale for their eleventh-hour assistance with the manuscript.

Finally, very special thanks to my wife, Alison, for all her love, patience, and support. (But mostly for her patience.)

CROSSHAIRS

CHAPTER ONE

The man in the sunglasses couldn't decide whether to kill or only maim. The many options available left a pleasant sensation in the pit of his stomach, not unlike the initial stages of sexual arousal.

He smiled and slid a bullet into the chamber of the sniper rifle, the brass cartridge clinking when it hit the hardened steel. The forearm of the customized Remington 700 rested on a sandbag, which in turn sat on a makeshift table assembled from pieces of scrap lumber he'd found downstairs. The table was set a few feet back from a square opening where a window would eventually be placed in the unfinished second-story bedroom.

The man shifted his rifle to the left, toward a large stucco residence across the street and down three lots. Like most houses on this block, it had been built in the past year, a gargantuan Mediterranean design on a too small, featureless lot, ostentatious and pathetic at the same time, jutting up from the flat Texas prairie.

He pushed the sunglasses up onto his forehead and squinted into the eyepiece of the Leopold scope. The details of the suburban yard sprang to life: the deep green of the chemically treated grass; the black mulch in the beds lining the front of the house; the yellow and red and blue of the flowers bursting from the plastic garden-center trays resting haphazardly on the lawn, waiting to be planted.

He eased his sunglasses back down and from a black duffel bag at his feet pulled out a handheld radio scanner. The device had been programmed with the frequencies for police and city services for Plano, Texas, the location of the house and this street. His employer was not without influence in certain government agencies and had made sure the frequencies were accurate. He turned on the scanner, set the volume to low, and placed a wireless earpiece in one ear.

Next, he removed a black plastic device about the size of a deck of cards. He extended a stubby antenna and switched on the power, making sure the LED indicator was lit.

The electronic instrument operated an extremely small and carefully placed explosive charge, designed to succeed if for some reason he chose not to use the rifle.

He ignored the smell of raw lumber and fresh plywood tickling his throat. He didn't know how long the wait would be, so he removed a small bag of organic cashews and ate a handful, keeping his attention focused on the house.

Fifteen minutes later, a figure appeared in the front yard.

The man removed his shades and peered through the scope. The optics brought the image into plain view: a tall, thin woman, olive-skinned, attractive, in her late thirties. She wore a pair of dirty khaki shorts and a faded, oversized red sweatshirt with the sleeves cut off.

The owner of the house.

The man nestled the butt of the Remington against his shoulder and placed his index finger on the trigger.

CHAPTER TWO

Dr. Anita Nazari wiped the perspiration from her face with the bottom of her red sweatshirt. She tried not to think about the e-mail and its implications, telling herself she was sweating from the heat of a Texas springtime, too intense after the past three years in Denver.

She grabbed a tray of petunias and began to work, placing each tiny container exactly an equal distance from its siblings, forming two perfectly parallel rows in the bed in front of her new house. The symmetry reminded her of test tubes in a rack.

Ordered and precise. Safe.

Anita picked up Container One, Row One and—with more force than intended—plunged the trowel into the moist earth, making a deep wedge-shaped hole. She squeezed the container until the roots slipped free from the sides, dropped the plant into the hole, and patted the dirt around the tiny stem. With a steady rhythm, she planted five more flowers and then stopped to wipe the sweat out of her eyes again.

Her heart was racing, her face slick and beaded. She could no longer pretend it was from the exertion. She had hoped the mindless activity would take her mind off the e-mail, but it hadn't.

She jumped at the sound of a throaty exhaust rumbling down the street.

Anita turned as the yellow Porsche Boxster belonging to Tom Maguire, her boyfriend of the past two months, stopped in front of her mailbox.

He got out, waved once, and approached.

Anita sat back on the grass and hugged herself.

"How's it goin—" Tom stopped, the smile slowly disappearing from his face. "What's wrong?"

"Nothing." Anita's voice was barely a whisper.

"Mira okay?" Tom looked toward the house. Mira was Anita's ten-year-old daughter.

"Yes." Anita nodded. "She's inside, doing her homework."

As if on cue, the front door opened and a gangly girl in jeans and a Britney Spears T-shirt stepped outside.

"Hey, Tom." The girl grinned, teeth too big for her head.

Tom smiled back. "Hey, kiddo."

"Your homework." Anita stood and tossed the trowel into the dirt as if it were a dagger. "Are you finished yet?"

"Almost." Her daughter sat down on the steps and yawned. "Long division sucks."

"Please go back inside and finish." Anita looked up and down the street. No cars that didn't belong were visible. "And don't use that kind of language."

"Wait till you get to algebra." Tom winked. "That *really* sucks."

They both laughed. Anita bit her lip and closed her eyes, trying to control the feeling of anger masking the helplessness rising like a bubble from her stomach.

"Mira." Anita's voice was tight and low. "Go inside. And finish your homework."

"C'mon, let her stay out here for a while," Tom said. "It's a gorgeous day."

Anita turned to her boyfriend, a happy-go-lucky former college football player who sometimes acted like he might have played one too many games without a helmet. She wondered if he had ever known true fear, the kind that makes your bowels watery and forces you to question the existence of anything but the evil humans do to each other. She wondered what it would be like to not know fear, to simply enjoy life and a sunny afternoon.

She tried to remember what things were like before the first e-mail. She couldn't.

CHAPTER THREE

The shooter in the second-story bedroom was known as the Professor in certain circles, the nickname derived from his ill-fated tenure as an instructor at Camp Peary, the CIA training facility also euphemistically known as the Farm. His current alias was unimportant, one of a dozen or more identifications he kept at the ready in safe locations accessible wherever an assignment took him.

The Professor ignored the arrival of the boyfriend, a minor obstacle that could be dealt with at his leisure. He kept the reticule of the scope centered on Anita Nazari but cranked the magnification back to widen the field of view.

The smell of the pine resin and the glues from the plywood was overpowering. He took shallow breaths, trying to keep his inhalation of the toxic fumes to a minimum.

While the doctor talked to the man from the yellow Porsche, the Professor looked away for a moment and pulled a leather case from his duffel bag.

The case contained an optical device that resembled a pair of binoculars with a headband attached, the latest in thermal imaging technology. He slipped the eyepiece over his skull and flipped on the unit, adjusting the sensitivity down almost as far as it would go. The sunny day disappeared, replaced by a surreal world of impressionistic colors: blue and gray with orange tints, the sidewalks and asphalt street appearing as hot red strips and the suburban lawns cooler and darker.

He stood in the middle of the bedroom and made a 360-degree sweep through the open framing, checking for any human-sized heat sources. Squirrels were oblong orange smudges, birds a tiny dab of pale pink.

Two doors down, an orange blob too small to be an adult but too large to be a dog seemed to be welded to a white-hot square slowly traversing the gray earth.

A neighbor kid was mowing the lawn.

The Professor was satisfied that no one was around who didn't belong. The chatter on Scanner One was minimal. He sat back down behind his makeshift bench and picked up the rifle.

The girl was on the front porch now, talking to the doctor and the man from the Porsche.

The Professor smiled.

Anita felt a needle in her temple, the stress headache arriving like the sudden thunderstorms that plagued the Texas prairie. Tom and Mira were talking, chattering on about some new television show on FOX featuring a group of California teenagers notable mainly for their grotesque wealth and promiscuity.

Mira reminded Anita of herself at the same age, the way she moved her hands when she talked, the angle of her head. Anita hoped her only child would never have to endure the same things that she had faced.

Anita thought again of the e-mail, and her stomach lurched.

"Mira," she said. "Please go inside and do your homework."

"Aw, Mom." Mira stood up.

Anita gave her the don't-mess-with-Mother look, one arched eyebrow over a steely gaze. Mira was a good child but needed guidance and reinforcement with certain things. Homework. Cleaning her room. And the maddening habit of talking to anybody at any time, no matter the inappropriateness of the circumstances, a proclivity Anita couldn't begin to understand. Strangers were to be feared, not conversed with.

"Hey, kiddo." Tom pointed to his car. "I've got those DVDs you wanted. Grab 'em before you go."

"Alllll riiight." Mira jumped up and headed to the Porsche.

The Professor saw the girl run toward the street, putting herself between a row of recently planted Bradford pear trees and the muzzle of the Remington. He kept the rifle in position but grabbed the remote control device.

As a field operative, he was allowed a certain latitude when it came to specific techniques. His employers wanted results. The details didn't matter.

He pressed the button.

Anita had closed her eyes and pinched the bridge of her nose between a thumb and forefinger when the explosion came, a low thump all the more threatening for its lack of intensity.

Mira screamed.

Anita opened her eyes and ran. She didn't see the bag of fertilizer and tripped, her forehead connecting with the turf.

Squeals of pain from her daughter, shouting from Tom.

"*Mira!*" She scrambled up. "I'm coming."

Tom was by the Porsche, a frantic look on his face. Mira huddled in a ball, near the curb.

Anita's senses weren't functioning correctly, her brain not processing data fast enough. She ran toward the two of them, the movement of her limbs agonizingly slow as if the air around her were heavy syrup.

Nothing made sense. Tom wasn't shouting; he was laughing. Mira's squeals sounded wrong, too, not painful anymore, happy now, full of excitement.

"Mira." She slid next to the child, embracing her in a protective clutch. "W-where are you hurt?"

"Mama, look." Her daughter held up a colorful plastic box marked with the familiar Apple logo. The latest-generation iPod, a must-have accessory for the middle-school set in Plano, Texas.

"What the . . ." Anita looked at the multicolored package and then at her daughter. "The blast?" She placed two fingers on Mira's carotid artery, felt a strong pulse. She looked for broken skin or protruding bones. Nothing.

"Anita?" Tom had stopped laughing. "What are you talking about?"

"Didn't you hear it?" Anita stood, full of anger now, and nowhere to direct it but at the man in front of her.

"Hear what?"

"There was an explosion." Anita looked around her yard. "I thought . . ."

"Oh, quit the act, for Pete's sake." Tom pointed to a cardboard container next to a pile of grass clippings sitting on the curb. A large jack-in-the-box was in the middle, its head swaying in the still air.

"What in the world?" Anita squinted at the toy. The pop-up part was a teddy bear, and its arms had been bent and cupped in the approximate size of an iPod box.

She quickly scanned the length of the block but saw nothing except her neighbor across the street in his front yard, chatting with the postman, both men smiling and laughing.

The music player must have popped out of the jack-in-the-box; the vast noise she'd heard had been her imagination.

"That was a great surprise." Tom stood and ruffled Mira's hair.

"Mommy, thank you thank you thank you." Mira squeezed her thin arms around her mother, the music player pressed between them. "I knew you didn't mean it when you said I couldn't have one."

"That was awfully spontaneous for you." Tom smiled. "Great idea, though."

Anita opened her mouth, but any words of substance died on her lips.

The message was clear. Nothing was safe. Ever. She wanted to tell Tom that she had never seen the cardboard box, nor the iPod. She wanted to tell him about the e-mails. But that meant committing a child's future to be a repeat of the mother's past. Which meant that Anita Nazari, MD, had precious few choices left.

She fought away the tears and did what any mother would do. She smiled and said, "Happy birthday, Mira."

CHAPTER FOUR

The Professor was satisfied with his work. Though the target would live another day, a message had been delivered, another layer of the operation complete. The stricken look on Anita Nazari's face, combined with the clueless laughter of the daughter and boyfriend, was perfect.

He turned off the remote control device and dropped it into the duffel bag along with the secondary scanner. He kept the earpiece for the radio in place on the slight chance that Nazari would contact the police.

The fumes from the particleboard siding, a mixture of formaldehyde and polyvinyl acetate glues, had made him light-headed, almost giddy.

He took shallow breaths and slipped the short-barreled sniper rifle into a protective case before placing it in the duffel and walking toward the hallway and the stairs leading to the first floor.

When he reached the bottom of the stairs, he stopped, realizing that he had not performed a final search with the thermal imager. The noxious odors had clouded his thinking. He cursed the weakness of his body.

Even as he grew angry at his mistake, he realized the risk was minimal. It was Sunday afternoon at a construction site where no workers were present nor would be for the foreseeable future. The builder had encountered unexpected financial problems, another fringe benefit of an employer with an extremely long reach.

The only danger would come from a nosy neighbor who might see him get into the ten-year-old pickup truck parked behind the privacy fence in the backyard. Even then, the chance of interference was small. Two removable magnetic signs on the doors of the truck were marked PLANO PLUMBING COMPANY. He was dressed in blue work clothes, a name tag on his breast that identified him as Kenny.

He adjusted the sunglasses, making sure they were secure on his face, and walked toward the back of the house.

When he was a few feet from the entrance to what would eventually be the kitchen, he smelled tobacco smoke and heard the heavy subflooring creak. Muffled voices sounded. He stopped and ran through the possible scenarios.

The local police.

Probability: low. He'd heard nothing on the scanner, and with dozens of homes under construction in this area, it was highly unlikely they would have stopped to check out this particular house. Also, police don't smoke as they investigate a potential crime scene.

Neighbors.

Probability: low to moderate. Though the infiltrators could be teens looking for a place to sneak a cigarette, this scenario didn't feel right. The people in the kitchen sounded heavyset, like construction workers, though that was impossible.

The Opposition.

Probability: impossible to calculate. Treat as high.

Anyone employed by the other side would be a professional, trained as he had been, maybe even one of his students from long ago. And professionals never smoked while working. On the other hand, the Professor had stayed alive as long as he had by treating the enemy with the utmost respect. Therefore, he decided to proceed as if the people in the next room were the Opposition.

He evaluated the situation. The work clothes he wore would buy him three or four seconds, all that was needed. He slouched his shoulders the way a tired plumber forced to work on a Sunday might do. He walked into the kitchen.

Two men stood there, tool belts slung over their shoulders, one holding a power saw and a bundled orange extension cord. They were beefy, on the edge of fit but not, in their midthirties, wearing the clothes of carpenters, heavy lace-up boots, worn Wrangler jeans, and T-shirts.

The Professor allowed himself to relax slightly. Construction workers. Why they were here, on a closed site, was another matter.

The one with the power saw was a little taller, maybe six-two, with reddish hair. He spoke first, a half-smoked cigarette dangling from his lips.

"You gotta work on a Sunday, too, huh?" His accent didn't match the clothes, not the typical Texas twang of a blue-collar worker. The syllables had a lilt to them, almost a brogue.

"Yes. Working on Sunday." The Professor dropped the duffel bag. It landed with a clank. He was now armed with only two weapons, a Microtech automatic knife clipped to his waistband and a SigArms .40-caliber handgun on his hip, covered by his untucked shirt.

The Sig didn't have a suppressor. Therefore, any action would require the silence of the knife.

"I thought this site was shut down." The second man frowned slightly when he spoke. "The owner said his contractor was screwing him. Nobody else was supposed to be here."

"Hey. What do I know?" The Professor smiled, trying to put the men at ease as he slipped closer.

"The plumbing's just stubbed in." Red Hair looked at the blank space where the kitchen sink would go. "What were you doing upstairs?"

The Professor estimated the distances and angles and knew he could neutralize both men. He hated deleting civilians, but the integrity of the mission was paramount.

In one smooth motion, he waved his left hand in a you're-not-gonna-believe-this gesture and moved toward the second man, the closer. He pulled the switchblade from his waistband.

Red Hair yelled and dropped the extension cord.

The Professor flicked the knife once across the throat of the second worker, jumping away before the blood spray got him, preparing to head for the next target.

Red Hair reacted quicker than expected. He threw the power saw, connecting with a glancing blow to the side of the Professor's head and knocking him to the floor.

The Professor's glasses fell off. The knife slipped from his grip.

Red Hair looked at his fallen partner and then at the assailant. "What the . . . ?"

The Professor shook his head a couple of times trying to clear the fog and double vision. He managed to grab the knife and stand up.

Red Hair scurried backward for a few feet until he tripped over a spool of electrical cord.

The Professor saw two identical figures sprawled on the floor. He made a choice and lunged toward the one on the left. He landed with a thud on an empty section of plywood flooring.

Red Hair was to his right, scrambling backward, swearing in a language the Professor had never heard before, though it seemed oddly familiar, like the man's out-of-place accent.

The Professor lashed out with the blade. Felt it slice through something soft. Heard a yell. He blinked several times until his vision returned more or less to normal.

Red Hair was limping as fast as possible across the backyard.

The Professor stood up. His vision went double again. He shook his head and worked his way to the rear entrance. When he looked in the backyard again, he saw the red-haired worker, blurry and indistinct like a mirage, holding on to his wounded leg.

He closed his eyes, took a deep breath. The veins in his legs throbbed, the result of the toxins in the air. When he opened his eyes he could see normally.

The backyard was empty.

From his breast pocket he pulled out another pair of sunglasses and put them on. He briefly evaluated his options and then began the cleanup process.

CHAPTER FIVE

Anita Nazari sat on a high-back bar stool, elbows resting on the dark gray granite countertop covering the island in the center of her kitchen. With one finger she idly traced the pattern in the polished stone, amazed at how important the choice of counters seemed only a few months ago.

She looked over to the Sub-Zero refrigerator where Tom Maguire stood, popping the tab on a can of Miller Lite. He took a long drink before walking to the island and sitting down next to her.

"How is your beer?" Anita arched one eyebrow and made a point of staring at the can.

"Jeez, Anita." The man sighed. "It's Sunday afternoon. The Rangers are gonna play in a little bit."

"Life is just one big game to you, isn't it?"

Tom had the beer halfway to his mouth but stopped. He put the can down on the counter. The sound of aluminum against rock was loud in the quiet kitchen.

"Suppose you tell me what's going on?"

"Never mind." Anita rubbed her temples. Even though he was attractive and attentive to her needs, she grew weary of Tom's simple and often clueless attitude toward life. She wondered why she spent so much time with him. The answer, as it always did, hit her like a spike in the chest.

Loneliness.

"You've sure been acting weird lately."

Anita imagined moving again, somewhere near the water. Maybe San Diego or Florida. Mira had always wanted to live by a beach. But they had moved too many times, a lifetime on the run, it seemed, and it wouldn't matter anyway.

"What time's the party tonight?" Tom drained the beer and tossed it like a basketball into the stainless-steel trash can a few feet away.

"There won't be any party this evening." Anita had planned a small get-together at Mi Cocina, a local Tex-Mex restaurant wildly popular with most of the neighborhood and Mira's school chums. After today, there was no way she was going to let a party happen.

"What are you talking about?" Tom had that slightly befuddled look that annoyed her so much.

"I wouldn't expect you to understand." Anita shook her head. She smelled her own sweat and the grass on her temple from when she had tripped over the bag of fertilizer. Her knee had suffered a minor abrasion and throbbed.

"You're unbelievable, you know that." Tom stood up.

"I-I'm sorry." Anita looked at him. "You need to give me a little time."

"Whatever the hell ever you want." Tom Maguire walked to the back door but stopped before leaving. He turned around. "Tell Mira happy birthday for me, okay?"

After Tom left, Anita placed a kettle of water on the front burner of the range and turned the flame to high. She pulled a chipped Wedgewood coffee cup from behind the row of gleaming mugs she'd bought at Pottery Barn.

The cup had originally been blue, but the years had dulled the intricate pattern to a pale gray. It was one of the last items she possessed that had belonged to her mother, and the only piece of china to survive all the midnight departures over the years.

She rinsed the heirloom in hot water before placing several grams of organic green tea into a stainless-steel infuser and easing the meshed device into the bottom of the cup. When the kettle whistled, she poured steaming water over the infuser, sniffing the aroma of fresh tea steeping.

The Dell laptop sat on the far counter, plugged into the same socket as the coffeemaker. Anita stared at the computer as she blew on her tea. The screen saver was a picture of Mira in her soccer uniform. She took a quick sip, burned her tongue slightly, and put the cup down. The room was suddenly chilly, but she no longer wanted any tea. She poured the remainder into the sink and carefully washed and dried the cup before returning it to its proper place.

When she was finished, she opened the refrigerator and removed a bottle of white Bordeaux. It was half empty; she and Tom had drunk a glass each the previous evening, to go with the rotisserie chicken she'd gotten from the grocery store.

She poured a large measure of wine into a crystal glass and walked over to the computer. She drank half of the wine in one gulp before clicking on her e-mail program.

The message was there, as she knew it would be.

She drained the glass and began to cry.

CHAPTER SIX

My name is Lee Henry Oswald, Hank to most people. I bear no kinship to the other Oswald, the man who changed the course of our nation's history so many years ago. My father was also named Lee Henry, and for reasons only he could articulate, he chose to bestow the moniker on his only son just a few years after President Kennedy met his grisly demise on the streets of Dallas.

In another time, I made my living as an investigator, a righter of wrongs, a would-be knight in rusted armor, the fix-it man of last resort for those greedy or vain or stupid enough to believe that riches and fame could be mined from the thin black soil of North Texas with only a winning smile and a trusting nature.

I was successful because these people soon found that the streets of Dallas were plated with a cheap layer of chrome, the hope of gold and silver and a never-sinking real estate market just so much spin from the chamber of commerce types. Except for the lucky few, the city promised diamonds but delivered rhinestones.

Dallas at the dawn of the new millennium was the land of leased luxury automobiles, zero-down, five-year interest-only loans, and a millionaire's lifestyle financed by the nice people at Visa.

I no longer operated as an investigator because I became like the people I served: vain and greedy and stupid enough to believe certain immutable physical laws did not apply to me.

I believed that a bad person could make a good choice, if only due to the force of my will.

I was wrong and people died. I lost my home, my place of business, and the needle to whatever moral compass I might at one point have possessed.

That was six months ago.

I tried for a while to carry on, but the edge was gone, my street radar damaged, a dangerous condition for one who dealt with dangerous people.

So I pared down what was left of my belongings and my expectations in life, and as my fortieth year on earth drew ever closer, I found work as a bartender at a chain restaurant next door to a multiscreen movie theater.

Now I served draft beer, margaritas, and watery drinks to men with BlackBerries on their belts and Mercedeses in the valet line, men who might or might not have been successful, and to tanned young women with silicone-enhanced chests who might or might not have been prostitutes.

Either way it was hard to tell, as the line between the dark and the light was so very thin. At any rate, the work was mindless and relatively stress free, a pleasant change from my former occupation.

The woman's name was Rhonda. She stood at the foot of my lumpy queen-sized bed in the Studio Six extended-stay motel near Dallas Love Field. She was in her late twenties, a Phoenix-based flight attendant for Southwest Airlines. She had a flight to Little Rock in two hours and would return later that afternoon.

At the moment she was wearing nothing but a black thong, a slim gold chain dangling between her perky breasts, and that slightly silly smile that women get when they start to cross the line from casually dating to being in a *R-e-l-a-t-i-o-n-s-h-i-p.*

Last night had been our fourth date and second time to sleep together.

She dug through her overnight bag and pulled out a bra that matched her panties. She put it on backward and then rotated it around to the proper position, a casual and intimate movement that never failed to fascinate me.

"About tonight, Hank." She maneuvered her left breast into its proper place inside the sheer black nylon.

"Tonight?" I sat up in bed and looked at the alarm clock.

"The party." She situated the right breast and then bent over and pulled a shirt from her bag. "At my friend Missy's house in Frisco."

"Oh yeah. That party." I rubbed my chin and tried to look thoughtful. Missy was another Southwest flight attendant. She lived in the suburbs of Frisco, Texas, a faraway land of cookie-cutter homes, PTA meetings, and strip malls with cutesy names like the Shoppes of this or that.

"I really want you to meet my friends." Rhonda shrugged on the shirt. "And Missy's husband has a construction company. It might be good for you to, you know, talk to him."

"Hmm." I got out of bed and stretched.

"Maybe see about getting a job." Rhonda crossed her arms. "You told me you didn't want to be a bartender for the rest of your life."

"Right. A job." I passed her on the way to the bathroom.

"I'm glad you're gonna go." Rhonda leaned against the door frame. "You'll really like everybody. And their house has this cool media room."

"Rhonda, here's the deal." I squeezed an inch of Colgate onto my toothbrush. "I'm supposed to work a double shift today."

"But you promised." She stuck out her bottom lip.

"Actually, I didn't." I turned on the tap and held the brush under the thin stream of water. "You assumed."

"So you're not going to the party with me?"

"No."

"I don't understand."

"I have to work."

"Okaaaaay." She nodded and got a confused look on her face, like there was too much data to process at one time. "Then when am I going to see you again?"

I shrugged in a noncommittal way and stuck the toothbrush in my mouth. This was clearly the wrong move.

"*What*?" She frowned and blinked several times. "You're not breaking up with me, are you?"

I made a noise through the mouthful of Colgate that could have been construed as "Of course not."

"I-I told my mother about you." She stomped her foot on the worn carpet.

I didn't reply, continuing with the teeth brushing instead.

Rhonda moved away from the bathroom and continued dressing. She was very quick now, no time for chitchat.

I rinsed out my mouth and stared at myself in the mirror. I hadn't worked out in months and it was starting to show. Six-three and muscular was slowly evolving into tall and heavyset, with thick in the middle not too far away.

The door slammed shut. I looked at the empty motel room, the rumpled sheets, soggy pizza boxes, and other accouterments of the transient existence, my home for the past few weeks, a constant, dingy reminder of the failures in my life.

I nodded at nothing and said, "Bye, Rhonda. See you real soon."

At ten fifty-nine I parked the elderly Nissan Maxima I was currently driving in the employee parking lot of a sports restaurant on Northwest Highway. I got out and put on my uniform, a multicolored apron complete with a name tag (Hank Oswald) and a pin advertising this week's specials (Long Island iced tea, pineapple-glazed chicken nuggets).

I clocked in at eleven oh-one, walked behind the bar, and checked the supply of beer in the coolers. We were getting low on Bud Light and Corona, so I made a notation on a form used to keep track of inventory.

I pulled a bag of limes and lemons out of the refrigerator, a knife and cutting board from underneath the bar.

My supervisor, a pimply-faced, pudgy guy in his early thirties named Felix, waddled up behind me, a clipboard in his hand. "Your spillage rate is high again," he said.

"Good morning to you, too." I sliced a lime in half.

"Up one-point-seven percent from last weekend." He tapped a piece of paper.

"Darn it. I was going for an even two percent. Gimme another try and I'll make it, promise." I smiled and cut half of the limes into wedges and dropped the pieces into a shallow white tray with a lid on top.

"Nobody likes a wiseass, Oswald." Felix put his chubby hands on his chubby hips. "Corporate keeps a close watch on these things, you know."

I halved a lemon. Felix loved to talk about all things corporate.

"There's a district manager position that's gonna open up in a few weeks." He made a note on his clipboard. "Our store's net revenue being what it is, I'm not gonna let a flake like you mess me up."

"You want to manage more of this?" I waved the kitchen knife at the empty bar, the big-screen television at the far end, the cheesy signs and decorations on the walls.

"I've got plans, Oswald." He leaned against the bar and stared at me. "More than I can say for you, always chasing women and stuff."

Several rebuttals came to mind, most involving the fact that Felix still lived with his parents, but I chose not to reply.

"Maybe if you didn't comp so many drinks for all the flight attendants that come in here . . ." Felix's voice trailed off as he wandered back to the kitchen.

I hit the next lemon so hard the cutting board flipped off the bar. Shaking my head, I turned around and threw the knife into the sink.

"Anger management classes not working out, huh?"

I turned toward the voice behind me. A very large man with shaggy blond hair stood on the other side of the bar, holding the board. He was wearing a pale yellow linen suit with a lavender silk shirt and had an unlit cigar stuck in his mouth.

His name was Olson, and he was at one time my closest friend. We'd gone to the edge of the world a time or two, broken bread with some very bad people and then killed them, and lived to talk about it. The last trip had been a little rough on Olson; his eye still drooped and his speech stuttered every so often from the blow to the head he received.

Because of me.

"You're a hard cat to locate these days." He put the board back on the bar. His movements and speech seemed more effeminate than the last time we had spoken months ago, right after he had split with his longtime life partner, a thug named Delmar.

"I'm taking a sabbatical." I got out another knife and grabbed a lemon.

"Got a proposition for you."

I shook my head.

"You just listen, don't talk." He smiled. "Tap your hand on the bar if you get confused."

"Olson . . ."

"Shhh." He held up one finger.

I sighed and slit the lemon in two.

"You remember Mike Baxter?"

I put the knife down. Mike Baxter had been in our Ranger unit during the first Gulf War. I nodded slowly.

Olson pulled a Zippo lighter out of his pocket and lit the cigar before speaking again. When there was a large cloud of blue smoke drifting toward the ceiling he said, "Mike's dying. And he wants you to find somebody for him."

I bit my bottom lip and frowned before shaking my head slowly. "Sorry, I'm not in the business anymore."

"Won't take long."

"Nope."

"It's Mike Baxter, for Pete's sake." Olson cocked his head to one side. "Do I have to spell it out for you? Brothers in arms. Blood oath, forged in combat, yadda yadda."

I started to reply but was cut off by Felix.

"What the heck is going on in here?" He was in the doorway leading to the kitchen, waving one hand in front of his face.

"Felix, give us a minute, will you?" I said.

"There's no smoking in here." He walked into the area behind the bar. "You gotta put that out now."

"We don't open for another twenty minutes." I looked at Olson and then back at my supervisor. "He'll be long gone by then."

Dallas had gone the way of New York and L.A., prohibiting smoking in all the fun places like bars and restaurants. On the other hand, it was never a good idea to tell Olson he had to do anything.

"You mean this guy is here to see you?" Felix crossed his arms.

"Is that a problem?" Olson's voice was soft, a danger sign.

"This is a place of work, Oswald. Not the homo social hour." Felix waved one fat hand at a man who'd saved my life on numerous occasions.

"What did you say?" I eased away from the beer taps and him, aware of the anger brewing in my chest.

Olson blew a smoke ring across the bar.

Felix said, "Your friend needs to put that out before I write you up."

"I asked you what you said. Something about a social hour."

"Uhh . . ." Felix frowned, the wheels turning inside his climb-the-corporate-ladder brain.

I grabbed him by the throat and stuck the point of the kitchen knife under his right eye, barely depressing the skin.

Felix made a noise like a mewing kitten.

"I think he's trying to talk." Olson sat down and plopped his elbows onto the bar.

"Anything you want to say?" I squeezed a little harder.

Felix managed a nod.

I eased the pressure on his larynx.

"S-s-sorry."

"About what?"

"W-what I said about your friend." Felix was sweating now, beads of perspiration dotting his florid face. "I'm sorry."

I let go and tossed the knife onto the bar.

Felix backtracked to the kitchen, one hand massaging his throat. When he got to the doorway he stopped and pointed a finger at me. "*You*—" A coughing fit interrupted his speech.

"Guess this means I won't be getting a quarterly bonus, huh?" I shrugged off my apron.

"—*are fired*." He was shaking now. "Out of here, before I call the police."

I walked around the bar to where my friend was still sitting, blowing smoke rings in the air. "Looks like you've got some free time now," Olson said.

CHAPTER SEVEN

The Professor awoke Monday as the gray light of dawn seeped into his sparsely furnished room. He had only managed a few hours of sleep in the dilapidated duplex in East Dallas, his base of operations that had been rented with cash several weeks before.

Disposing of the body yesterday had proven problematic, complicated by the sudden appearance of a group of children in the alley as he was about to drive away with the corpse hidden in the back of the pickup. Hours had been lost, time that could have been better spent searching for the second contractor.

Curiously, the man he'd already eliminated had possessed no ID in his wallet nor any credit cards, only a wad of currency and a handful of business cards for his contracting company. A quick database search of the man's name and address yielded little, and what information it did turn up was conflicting.

Could the two men have been something other than simple carpenters?

The Professor contemplated heading to the address on the card, a few dozen kilometers west of his current location. He mulled over his options, like a wizened lion circling his prey.

The address was too risky for the moment, at least without additional information, information best obtained from the site of initial contact. He would return to Plano after the scheduled check-in with his employer.

He slid out of bed and decided to run through his regular routine, a series of isometric exercises, followed by thirty minutes with a set of free weights and another half hour of jumping rope.

He performed his workout in the empty and un-air-conditioned garage behind the duplex, with the doors and windows shut. When he was finished, perspiration dripped from his body, dotting the cement floor. He smiled. Sweating forced the toxins from the system.

He returned to the kitchen and consumed a liter of spring water, followed by a small bowl of organic granola topped with unpasteurized goat's milk he had bought from the health food store a few blocks away.

After finishing, he pulled from the pantry a large cardboard box containing dozens of vitamin bottles. Due to the time spent in the house in Plano and the toxins there, he increased his dosage of antioxidants: vitamin C, vitamin E, coenzyme CQ-10, and magnesium citrate. The capsules filled a small juice glass to the midpoint. He washed them all down with more spring water.

After putting away the vitamins, he took a quick shower and dressed in khakis, a nondescript plaid shirt, and rubber-soled moccasins. He slipped a small-framed Glock nine-millimeter in his rear pocket and a fresh switchblade in the front of his waistband, the overhang from the shirt hiding its tiny clip from anything but the closest scrutiny. The knife used yesterday had gone down a sewer grate miles away.

He left the duplex and walked to the west, passing the tidy brick bungalows that made up much of this part of the city and reminded him of the Silver Lake section of Los Angeles. Prior to his arrival, he'd learned that many people in this part of Dallas were bohemians, artists and musicians and other transient types, the perfect demographic for one wishing to blend in.

After two blocks, he headed south on Greenville Avenue, a major nightlife district in the region. The buildings on either side of the street housed clubs and restaurants, but most were closed at this hour on a Monday morning. He encountered very few people, mostly Hispanic workers performing cleaning chores.

He stopped at a pay phone in front a garishly decorated place called the Whiskey Bar and dialed a toll-free number he'd memorized weeks before. The signal went to a call center in Miami, where it was routed to another subterranean switching station somewhere in the Midwest; the Professor didn't know where, nor did he care to.

After a few seconds, the phone on the other end was answered and the voice of his employer came on the line.

"Yes."

"It's me."

"Well, hello, sugar." The woman sounded like she'd been raised in the South somewhere, maybe Alabama, the simple sentence drawn out and languid. "How *is* my order coming?"

The Professor waited while a bus rattled by. He tried not to breathe in the diesel exhaust.

"Are you there?"

"Yes." The Professor tried to imagine what she looked like. A southern belle with eyes that sparkled when she laughed but displayed little emotion otherwise. "Everything is progressing as planned."

"Progressing?" she said. "I was expecting fulfillment."

"That will be this week." The Professor's brow grew damp, not from the heat.

"Of course," the woman said. "That's what we ordered, right?"

"I don't like to check in like this." The Professor mopped his brow with his sleeve as a police car glided down the street.

The woman sighed. "We're paying the bill, sugar."

"I need to go."

"All right, then . . ." Her voice drifted away, as if she were talking to someone else in the room with her. "Hold on a sec, okay?"

The Professor blinked sweat out of his eyes. Another police unit idled down the street.

"New info." She came back on the line.

"Yes?"

"No more contact with the subject until you hear from me."

"What?" The Professor was incredulous. "What about surveillance?"

"There are issues that you are not aware of." The woman's voice had lost a little of its southern charm.

"I thought you understood. I don't work this way." The Professor tried not to sound too incredulous.

"You came highly recommended," the woman said. "It would be a shame to report back otherwise."

The Professor started to reply but realized she had hung up. He placed the phone back on the cradle and walked away, planning the most covert method to get to Plano in the next few hours.

CHAPTER EIGHT

We headed south on Interstate 35 in Olson's new four-door Maserati, toward where Mike Baxter lay dying at the Dallas VA Hospital. I asked about the Jaguar he'd been driving the last time we were together. Olson laughed and said he'd done several very lucrative deals in the past few months. Something about a couple of thousand North Korean AK-47s and a guy from Florida. I didn't ask anything else.

I had left the elderly Maxima in the parking lot of my place of former employment. The title wasn't in my name, and the chassis had almost rusted away; Felix could have it as a parting gift.

The freeway ran past the glass-and-steel skyline of Dallas. The Texas School Book Depository, made infamous by my namesake, was briefly visible as we drove by American Airlines Center and the new W Hotel tower. The county jail was on the other side of the highway, existing in an uneasy symbiosis with the rest of the city.

After another couple of miles the Maserati crossed the bridge leading into South Dallas, forty feet above the Trinity River, a thin stream of muddy water that divided the city into two separate but unequal halves. The downtown glitz, the sports arena, and most of the wealth resided north of the river. The south half was populated by people in the lower income brackets, immigrants legal and otherwise, and those that preyed on the recent arrivals—the grifting class, as I liked to think of them.

The Dallas VA was on South Lancaster, a gleaming brick building more than a little incongruous with its surroundings: check-cashing liquor stores, tiny bodegas offering phone cards to Mexico, and used car lots.

Olson pulled in at an angle at the far end of visitor parking, taking up two spots. Before he got out of the car, he pulled a Colt Commander from behind his hip and placed it in the console.

"Sometimes they have the metal detectors set up." He pushed the driver's door shut, chirped the alarm. "You carrying?"

I shook my head. "Haven't touched a gun in months."

"Used to be you wouldn't go to the bathroom without a Browning Hi-Power strapped somewhere."

"Times change." I headed toward the front entrance, a solid quarter of a mile away.

The long sidewalk leading to the hospital was like a concrete river filled with former servicemen of all ages and colors, with varying degrees of mobility.

The farthest away from the facility were the youngest, vets from the latest Middle East conflict. Most were in wheelchairs and were missing limbs. I nodded a hello to a young Hispanic man who was probably not yet old enough to drink. He'd sacrificed a lot for Uncle Sam, including two legs, one arm, and any chance of ever sleeping without dreaming of the utter obscenity that is the battlefield.

The next group was roughly my age, clustered on either side of forty, soldiers and sailors from the era of the first Gulf War. Not many missing limbs among these, but I knew all too well they suffered from the dream also.

The last group was huddled around the entrance, one big mass of older, smoking men, IV bottles and catheter bags perilously attached to wheelchairs. These were the vets who had served in Vietnam and Korea, a paunchy, gray-haired, hollow-eyed mass of humanity waiting for the final quarter to end. A few of the oldest ones had no doubt served in World War II.

I smiled and nodded where appropriate and stepped inside the building into a three-story atrium. More men in wheelchairs and medical personnel in scrubs, moving slowly across the polished granite floor.

"Depressing, isn't it?" Olson stood beside me.

"Where are we going?" I wanted in and out as fast as possible.

"Fifth floor." Olson headed toward a bank of elevators. "Oncology."

After a long wait, we boarded an elevator, following several men in wheelchairs. The man closest to me had an uncontrollable tremor in his left arm.

At the fifth floor we got off, Olson leading the way to the nurses' station. The air was heavy with bleach and cleansers that tried but failed to cover the sickly odor of decay. He had a whispered conversation with a stern-looking woman in navy blue scrubs before turning my way and pointing to a partially opened door across the hall.

"Let's go." He walked into the room, and I followed.

The last time I had seen Mike Baxter was about ten years ago, at the St. Patrick's Day parade on Greenville Avenue. He'd been his usual jovial self, a burly, fun-loving guy, laughing, drinking green beer from a plastic cup. He'd told me about his new wife and his new job, selling cars at a Chevy dealership in Garland. Life was good for Mike Baxter. We'd made the usual promises to keep in touch.

Now only his eyes were the same, a pale blue like the spring sky after a good hard rain.

The rest of his body belonged to a different person, gaunt as a death camp inmate, skin splotchy and pale. He smiled wanly when I said hello, lifting one skinny arm in a wave. His other limb was tethered to a grove of IV bags.

"Good to see you, Hank." He pointed to a chair by his bed. "Have a seat, why don't you?"

I sat. Looked at his thin legs underneath the blankets. Figured he couldn't weigh more than 120 or 130, tops. We were about the same height, six-three or so. I clocked in at an even 200.

Olson moved to the window and stared out over the parking lot.

"Mike," I said. "How are you doing?"

He raised one eyebrow and looked around the room but didn't say anything.

"What's, uh . . . wrong?" As I remembered, he was three or four years older than I was, but he looked like he was seventy.

"Cancer is the latest thing." Mike closed his eyes. "But it started when we got back. I had migraines like you wouldn't believe."

I nodded. A lot of vets had come back from Iraq and Kuwait with headaches and other symptoms. The docs had given it a name, the so-called Gulf War Syndrome, though the Pentagon and the VA insisted the problem was mental. Any physical issues were an aberration, kind of like the effects of Agent Orange on an earlier generation of American warriors.

"I need your help," Mike said.

I leaned forward in the chair. A stale, metallic odor emanated from his wasted body.

"My daughter." He grabbed my hand. "I haven't seen her since she was in the first grade."

"How old would she be now?"

"Turned twenty-one last month." He coughed, phlegm rattling deep in lungs. "I-I want to see her before I die."

"Here's the situation." I nodded slowly. "I'm not doing the PI thing right now."

Mike stared at the ceiling. His breathing was shallow and ragged. After a few minutes he looked at me again.

"You remember January 1991?" he said. "A Monday morning."

I didn't reply. I looked over at Olson, who was studiously ignoring me.

"The oil field fire?" Mike said.

"I remember." I kept my tone even.

"They'd rigged the wells to blow when we got close."

I nodded.

"I've never seen anything like it." Mike grabbed an oxygen tube hanging on the railing of his bed and put the apparatus around his head. "The smoke was purple."

"It looked like a black cloud from base," I said.

"It wasn't." He shook his head. "Not if you were there. It was a purple haze."

No one spoke for a few minutes. Olson wandered out to the hallway, leaving us alone.

Mike coughed again. "But you didn't see it up close, did you?"

"No." My voice was a whisper.

"The smoke was everywhere, like a fog."

I got up and walked to the window.

"You didn't go that day, remember?" Mike sat up in bed. "I went in your place."

I turned back around.

"Her name is Susan Baxter. I've written down her particulars." He held out a slip of paper. "Find her. Bring her to me."

I walked to his bed, took the information, and left.

CHAPTER NINE

The Professor shot the man in the back of the head. The metallic clank of the slide was the only sound that emanated from the silenced Ruger. He dragged the body behind the Ford Five Hundred, opened the trunk, and saw that the compartment was packed with boxes and blister packs containing capsules.

Pharmaceutical samples. Giveaway containers of a popular allergy medicine. The man had been a drug rep.

The Professor shook his head at the irony of it all and wrestled the corpse inside the trunk before shutting it.

The alley was empty.

He hurried to the driver's seat. He had waited a long forty minutes behind the Starbucks on Greenville Avenue for the right person to come along, someone in a late-model car, a professional type traveling alone.

He'd disposed of the pickup from yesterday, and new transportation wasn't due to arrive until tomorrow. He could have rented a car using the set of fake credentials he'd been provided, but his employer would know as soon as the credit card data hit the information grid. He could have stolen a parked car, but the theft would have been reported, maybe not for a while, but still an unacceptable risk. Thus, logic dictated the action he took.

Because he had to get back to Plano and begin the process of finding the second contractor.

The witness.

CHAPTER TEN

I found Olson by the nurses' station, talking on his cell phone, something about a pallet of M1 carbines. He held up one finger, motioning for me to wait.

I leaned against the wall next to a fire extinguisher and looked at the piece of paper Mike had given me.

Susan Baxter. Last known address was her mother's home in Fort Worth. A scribbled note at the bottom that she'd been a sophomore at TCU last year. Finding her would take fifteen minutes using a couple of databases. Getting her to the Dallas VA might be a different matter.

A moan from a room next door to Mike Baxter's. I tried not to shudder, envisioning myself as a patient here, dependent on the sometimes-adequate, sometimes-not care of Uncle Sam.

A small group of people in white lab coats emerged from the room. An Indian male spoke in a thick accent to a woman as he scribbled on a clipboard. They moved in the way doctors do, imperious, trailing subordinates like celebrities with an entourage. The male doctor appeared to be seeking the approval of the woman, glancing at her every few steps as they approached Mike Baxter's room.

The group stopped at the entrance to Mike's room, where my friend lay dying. The woman pulled a beeper from her hip and walked away, dodging the traffic in the hallway. The Indian doctor watched her go. After a few moments, he shrugged and entered the room.

The woman ended up on the other side of the fire extinguisher from me, a cell phone in one hand, beeper in the other. She was tall, at least six feet in her heeled boots, and attractive, with a prominent nose and high cheekbones under skin the color of coffee ice cream.

But her eyes were puffy, ringed in dark circles like the eyes of an intern suffering from lack of sleep, out of place with her age, which I put at around forty.

She snapped her phone shut and turned to me. "Why do men think it's acceptable to openly stare at a woman?"

I shrugged. "Beats watching guys die." Olson was still by the nurses' station, jabbering on his phone.

"Why are you here?" She had a faint accent I couldn't quite place. "You don't look sick."

"I'm visiting someone."

"Oh." She sounded confused, as if the concept were foreign. "Who?"

"An old army buddy." I pointed to Mike Baxter's room.

"He's going to die," she said. "You are aware of that, aren't you?"

"How do you know?" I tried not to get angry at her matter-of-fact attitude.

"Gulf War vet. Cancer complicated by ALS." She shook her head.

"Nice talking to you." I pushed away from the wall with one hand. "You might want to work on the bedside manner, though."

"*What?*"

I ignored her and walked up to Olson.

He snapped his phone shut. "Well, did you take the job?" He headed toward the elevator.

"How could I say no?" I followed him.

"*Stop.*"

We both turned around, as did everyone else in the hall. The doctor I'd been talking to stood there, finger pointing at my chest.

Olson shook his head. "Why do you piss off people everywhere you go?"

The woman approached. Her dark brown eyes were no longer tired, anger replacing the fatigue. Two burly orderlies stood behind her, arms crossed, doing the tough-guy thing.

"Do you know who I am?" She stopped a foot away from us. Her face was flushed.

"Marcus Welby's love child?" I turned to Olson. "Let's get out of here."

"Wait." The woman grabbed my arm.

"Don't touch me." I kept my voice low.

One of the orderlies moved closer. "The doctor's not done talking to you."

"Shouldn't you be cleaning out a bedpan or something?" Olson's smile was tight across his face. The orderly took a step back.

I placed my hand over the woman's and removed it from my arm.

"I am trying to help these people," she said, "and you dare accuse me of being insensitive."

"I'm trying to help, too." I turned and pressed the down button. "One in particular. The guy you said is gonna die."

"I . . . I'm sorry."

"Why?" I got on the elevator with Olson.

The woman opened her mouth, but the doors closed before she could reply.

Let me guess," Olson said. "Somebody you used to date? Maybe did the old hump-and-dump on her?"

"Why didn't you tell me what he looked like?" I punched the button for the lobby.

The elevator stopped on the third floor, and he didn't reply. Two elderly men wheeled themselves on. They smelled like Listerine and hair tonic. On the ground floor, I held the door open as they exited.

When they had rolled off I said, "Told you I don't want to get back in the life."

"What are you gonna do, then?" He stopped in the middle of the lobby and put his hand on my shoulder, a stream of invalid soldiers coursing around us. "Tend bar at Hooters? Sell used cars?"

"Maybe." I looked at the tile floor.

"Right." He walked away, headed to the front door. After a few moments, I followed him outside. The humidity had gotten worse, the sky gray with thunderclouds.

We stood together at the entrance, looking over the sweep of lawn leading toward Lancaster Street, each blade of grass perfectly manicured courtesy of the American people's tax dollars.

"You need to snap out of this, Hank." Olson pulled a cigar from his pocket and lit it. "Get your act together."

"I had it all working before and look what happened," I said. "How are your headaches these days?"

"That wasn't your fault." He headed down the sidewalk but stopped and turned after a few feet. "You coming with me?"

"I'll catch the bus."

He raised one eyebrow.

"Leave me alone, willya?"

"Suit yourself." My friend shook his head. "It's a missing person case, take you a day or so. Quit acting like a bitch." He walked away.

I sat down on a bench and stared at a cigarette butt on the ground. Geezers wheeled past. After a few minutes, I became aware of someone standing in front of me.

"I was talking to you." The woman from the fifth floor stood there, arms crossed.

"It's not been the best of days. Why don't you leave me alone."

"My name is Anita Nazari." She sat down next to me.

"Shouldn't you be doctoring or something?"

"Your friend told me you are an investigator." She crossed her legs and stared at the traffic on Lancaster. "A very good one even though you are named for an assassin."

"Don't believe everything you hear." I ignored the Lee Harvey reference; that got easier to do with age.

"He said you can do what others can't."

I stood up and walked down the sidewalk toward the street. The woman followed, the heels of her boots clicking on the concrete.

"Please stop."

I turned around and faced her.

"I need someone to help me." Her eyes were filled with tears, the anger gone.

"I'm not in the helping business anymore." I could feel the panic coming off her in waves.

"Please, at least listen to me?"

I closed my eyes. A trickle of sweat slid down my forehead. I thought about how much I didn't want to ride the bus. I had nowhere to go anyway.

"Can you give me a ride?"

"What?"

"You can tell me what your problem is while you drive."

"Of course." She nodded once, all businesslike. "Where do you want to go?"

"Not sure right now." I headed toward the parking lot. "I'll tell you when we get there."

CHAPTER ELEVEN

The Professor ignored the blare of the rap music coming from the open windows of the Lincoln Navigator stopped next to him at the light. He did not return the stares of the two young African American males sitting low in the seats of the luxury SUV.

He kept his eyes straight ahead, hands gripped on the steering wheel of the stolen Ford Five Hundred, trying to convey the image of a scared, midlevel, middle-aged managerial type who had taken a wrong turn. He'd spent the last ten minutes looking for a tail—"dry cleaning," the Agency spooks used to call it. Driving in random loops, alternating his speed, making sudden turns, standard automobile protocol designed to reveal if anyone was following. His trip to the cleaners had been successful; no one was tailing him.

The light changed.

The Lincoln didn't move.

The Professor accelerated slowly and headed south on Parry Avenue. A few seconds later, the Navigator pulled away from the intersection and slid in behind him.

He shook his head and wished that the young men in the SUV would not follow. They weren't professionals, most probably just bored youths looking for someone to mess with, and he didn't want to hurt them. He didn't want to hurt anybody. He just wanted to do his job and be left alone.

He was on the northern fringes of the Fair Park area, a pie-shaped wedge of clapboard houses and weed-infested lots a few miles east of downtown Dallas, the area named for the Art Deco–styled fairgrounds to his left, according to his research.

An operative in a strange city always has two places from which to work. A main base, in this instance the rented duplex in the bohemian yet still middle-class neighborhood near Greenville Avenue.

And a safe house.

A *smart* operative doesn't tell his employer about the second site, the backup location, in case something goes wrong or carefully arranged plans suddenly become fluid for whatever reason. Even though his employer had no reason to doubt that he would follow her orders, nor the Opposition any reason to be aware of his presence, the Professor had learned over the years to trust his instincts.

Right now, his instincts told him to avoid his main base for the time being.

The Professor's safe house was a rented room above a bar a few blocks from the Texas state fairgrounds. The immediate area was full of rusting warehouses and machine shops sitting next to tattoo parlors and taverns favored by edgy young people looking for an urban experience in a quintessential suburban city.

This section of Dallas was also where the black and white populations came together, sort of a no-man's-land offering unique opportunities to remain out of sight while hidden in plain view.

He turned right on Exposition Avenue, a street lined with ancient brick buildings, some faded and battered like a forgotten old uncle, others glossy with fresh paint that did little to hide the true age and condition of the underlying structure.

The Navigator and its thumping bass passed him as he parked in an empty spot on the street. A building, which apparently had been newly renovated into loft apartments, was to his right. It didn't look very apartmentlike or inviting, with the steel roll-up door blocking the garage entrance and the razor wire topping the brick wall.

The Professor turned off the ignition and looked at the snapshot taped to the dashboard. The picture had been taken at a restaurant: a man and a woman in their midthirties and two young girls, maybe five or six years old.

Twins, he surmised from their near-identical resemblance as well as the pair of packages covered in pink birthday wrapping in the backseat addressed to Holly and Hailey.

In a moment of uncharacteristic indulgence, he allowed himself to feel a vague sense of distaste at the bottom of his stomach, a few milliliters of compassion or grief for the family fabric he had ripped to shreds because of circumstances beyond his control.

The Professor slipped a finger under his sunglasses and wiped his cheeks before ripping the picture from the dashboard, his eyes watery, probably the formaldehyde seeping from the interior material of the newish car. He stepped outside and tossed the photo into the gutter.

The Navigator drove by again, going the opposite direction. Both young men stared at him with flat eyes that swiveled in their sockets as their heads stayed forward.

He ignored them and jogged across the greasy asphalt of Exposition Avenue.

The bar occupied the ground floor of a three-story building. A rusted fire escape ran along the side of the structure, the stairs ending a dozen feet above the parking lot of a transmission shop.

He pushed open the door and let the peculiar odor from a combination of alcohol, stale smoke, and commercial disinfectant wash over him. He tried not to cough.

The drinking establishment was one big room. Mismatched furniture, darkened wood floors, signs advertising obscure central European ales dotting bone-colored walls. The ceiling was older than the women's suffrage movement, made from hammered tin grimy with dirt.

It was near midday, and the only person in the room was a woman by the cash register wearing a black T-shirt with ANARCHY emblazoned in red across the front. Her skin was albino white.

"Hey," she said. "Can I help you?"

A retro-style Wurlitzer jukebox sitting by the mahogany bar clicked on and a Buck Owens song began to play.

"A beer would be nice." The Professor didn't drink alcohol but sat down on a stool anyway. Bartenders knew the comings and goings in a neighborhood. A few moments of conversation might be beneficial.

"What kind?" She lit a cigarette and blew a jet of smoke into the empty room, right past the Professor's head.

"Do you have anything organic?" He tried to keep his breathing shallow.

"Sorry." She smiled. "We're fresh out of Tree Hugger Lager."

"Oh, well. I must be going anyway." The Professor covered his mouth and coughed before he held up a key. "I'm in Unit A."

"Sure. See you later, then." She twisted one of the rings in her nose.

The Professor walked to a small alcove at the rear of the bar. The two doors on the left smelled like urine and pine cleaner. The one on the right opened onto a tiny landing. Stairs led upward toward the rear of the building.

He took them two at a time and stopped when he reached the top, pausing to listen for any noise or movement. A narrow hallway was in front of him, three or four doors on either side.

At the far end of the corridor, an exit door opened and the passenger from the Lincoln Navigator stepped out. He wore a Dallas Mavericks ball cap and a white ribbed undershirt.

"Yo." The man wasn't as young as he'd looked in the SUV.

The Professor smiled and nodded. His room was the first one on the left. He headed that way.

"They told me to watch out for you." The man moved like a leopard down the hallway, fluid, stalking.

"I think you have me confused with somebody else." The Professor shrugged and raised his eyebrows in confusion. He stopped at his door, still trying for the befuddled-suburban-white-guy effect.

"One large." The man pronounced "large" as "larch."

"I-I'm sorry. I don't understand." The Professor put the key in the dead bolt but kept his attention focused on the man a few feet away.

"Said they'd gimme one lar—I mean one thousand." He stuck his right hand in the front pocket of his oversized jeans. "A thousand bucks for me to call if somebody that looks like you shows up on my streets."

"Looks like me?" The Professor frowned and flipped the lock.

"Yeah." He nodded. "Old white-bread dude, glasses."

"You definitely have the wrong fellow. No one ever looks for me." The Professor wrinkled his face in a sheepish grin and pushed the door open but didn't enter. He was surprised but strangely content. Someone knew about him and had made inquiries in various parts of town where he might have a safe house.

They were presenting a challenge. The stakes were higher than he'd been told.

"You give me two grand and I forget I've seen you." The man held out his free hand.

"Two thousand dollars?" The Professor took a half step back. "Surely this is a joke of some sort."

"You saying there's something funny about me?" The man frowned. "I need two large from—"

The Professor crushed the thug's windpipe with his fist.

The man grabbed his throat and wheezed. He bounced from wall to wall like a hyperactive pinball, making more noise than was acceptable under the circumstances.

The Professor snatched an arm and pulled him into the tiny unfurnished room, closing the door quietly. He eased the man down to the floor and watched as he died, his body slowly stopping the struggle for the oxygen that would never come.

After a few moments, the Professor went to the window-mounted air conditioner and pulled off the intake grill. From a small slot underneath the condenser unit, he removed a manila envelope wrapped in plastic and opened it.

Three sets of ID. Driver's licenses. Credit cards. Insurance information, even movie rental and library cards. Also passports, two American, one Irish. And the maximum amount of cash that could be carried and not attract the attention of the authorities in case of a search: $9,950 in used, high-denomination bills.

From the closet on the other side of the room, he removed several sets of clothing, each different in style and cost. He stuffed them, along with the envelope, into a small duffel bag.

Next, he went to the freestanding gas space heater in the bathroom and removed a Sig Sauer .40-caliber taped underneath the bottom. He slipped that into the bag, too.

Before leaving, he took a last look at the man on the floor. Dead, unseeing eyes stared at the stained plaster ceiling.

The Professor headed to the stairs.

The driver of the SUV sat at the bar, a bottle of Stella Artois in front of him. He and the girl in the ANARCHY T-shirt looked up as the Professor stepped into the room. No one else was present.

The Professor pulled the silenced Ruger from his waistband and shot the African American in the forehead.

The bullet, a high-velocity .22 hollowpoint, didn't penetrate the man's skull, an unfortunate side effect of using a small-caliber cartridge that could be silenced easily. The man stayed standing, eyes open and staring in confusion as a tiny stream of blood trickled down his face.

The Professor fired again, the bullet striking just to the left of the man's nose. The target dropped to the floor, the beer he'd been drinking falling over on the bar with a clink almost as loud as the suppressed gunshot.

The bartender gulped. Her mouth opened in a wide, perfect circle.

The Professor fired again.

CHAPTER TWELVE

Anita Nazari's hunter green Range Rover breezed through the northbound booth leading onto the Dallas Tollway, the pay-as-you-go highway that split the top half of the city in two.

I was in the passenger seat, watching the concrete slide by. We hadn't spoken since leaving the hospital parking lot. I hadn't even told her where to take me, and she hadn't asked.

Most women would agree that I'm no expert when it comes to the emotions of the fairer sex. Even so, I sensed Dr. Nazari's mood as very dark. The clues were all there. Stifled crying. Muttered curses at slow-moving traffic. Excessive horn use.

"What kind of doctor are you?" I said.

"I have enough money." She swerved into the far left lane and jammed her boot on the accelerator. "You'll be paid."

"If I take the job."

No response. She turned on the CD player and the interior of the luxury auto filled with what sounded like Gregorian chant.

"Nice tunes." I fiddled with the seat controls until the back reclined a few inches.

"I'm a researcher. I specialize in immunological disorders."

"Oh."

"Do you know about fear, Mr. Oswald?"

"Call me Hank."

"Avoiding the question, are we?" A faint smirk crossed her face.

I avoided the urge to make a smart-ass response. I did in fact know quite a bit about being afraid. Fear was good, if you could manage it. Fear gave you an edge, that extra dose of adrenaline that could keep you off the coroner's slab.

However, I sensed that fear was managing Dr. Nazari, not the other way around.

"Where are you from?" I said.

"What does that have to do with anything?"

"Why don't you drop me off at the next exit." I returned the seat to its original position.

"No, please."

I didn't say anything.

"I was born in Tehran." She turned down the volume of the music as we passed the glass towers clustered at Preston Center. The traffic began to grow heavier as lunchtime approached.

"When did you get out?"

"My family left two years after the shah fell, 1981." Her tone of voice changed, the hostility replaced by something like resignation.

"Must not have been a pleasant time."

"No." She shook her head slowly. "From one dictator to another. You can't imagine."

I reached over and turned off the music. "Why do you need somebody like me?"

She didn't speak for a mile or so. Then, "The first e-mail came about a year and a half ago."

I nodded.

"It said, 'Sophie must die.' I didn't think anything of it. Lots of strange people out there, you know?"

"Sure."

"The next day I returned home and found my daughter's favorite doll in *my* bathroom, its head ripped off." She took several deep breaths before continuing. "In the context of the e-mail, the name meant nothing to me."

"I don't follow."

"My daughter's doll. She'd called it Sophie."

We were both silent for a few moments.

"Who had access to the house?" I said.

"No one." She looked at me for a second before returning her attention to the traffic. "The next e-mail came maybe a month later, from the same address. It read, 'Hello.'"

"That's all?"

"Yes."

"And then?"

"Another few months go by." She switched lanes and accelerated past a BMW ragtop. "A cryptic reference to a certain chemical substance. Again I failed to place the significance."

I waited for her to continue.

"An experiment in my lab, ruined. The data was backed up, of course, but a point had been made."

"Nothing is safe," I said.

"Yes. A common theme in my life, I'm afraid."

"What sort of research do you do?"

"You wouldn't understand."

"Try me. I was awake for most of my tenth-grade biology classes."

"In the past my work concerned the molecular interactions between lymphocyte receptors and their ligands." She sighed and ran a hand through her hair. "After that I designed a protocol for experimenting with the prion agents of the transmissible spongiform encephalopathies."

"Wow." I whistled once. "That was *you* that did that thing with the sponges?"

"Yes." She sounded perplexed. "I'm surprised you've heard of the process. It's very technical—"

I held up a hand. "I was joking. I didn't understand a word you said."

The smile that had been forming on her face disappeared.

"Let me ask the same question a different way," I said. "Is there a lot of competition in what you do? Anybody out there trying to stop you from succeeding?"

"No. Much to the chagrin of my employers, there's little interest in my work."

We rode in silence for a few miles.

"What do they want?" I said. "Do they ask for anything?"

"That's the worst part." She maneuvered around a Suburban full of kids, a harried-looking blonde behind the wheel, talking on a cell phone. "They never say."

The cloud cover increased the farther north we went, an ugly blue-gray swath like bruises on the battered sky.

"Another one came two days ago," she said. "It concerned my daughter. A gift was delivered for her birthday. Rather unexpectedly." She explained the details. I asked a few questions and quickly figured that the person initiating the action had to be close by, using a remote control of some sort. Too risky that the device might have been set off by a passerby.

Neither of us spoke for a while. The traffic slowed more as we got to the LBJ Freeway, the inner loop of the city, an eight-lane, perpetually clogged highway bordered on each side by office towers and shopping malls.

We were slowed behind a Dodge minivan, the back of which was plastered with stickers for a nondenominational church in southern Dallas County that allegedly had ten thousand members.

Anita Nazari pushed a shock of dark hair out of her face and looked at me. Her eyes were wide but betrayed nothing. "Will you help me?"

I returned her stare. "I'm out of the business."

"My daughter is ten years old."

"What about her father?" I said. "Most things like this are traceable to a disgruntled ex-spouse."

"My husband died a long time ago." She paused. "He was in your special forces. All I know is that it was combat, in the Middle East somewhere."

I didn't say anything. The image of Mike Baxter dying in a cramped hospital bed scrolled across my mind. I thought about a girl growing up without a father to protect her.

The traffic eased and we drove past the Galleria shopping mall.

"You were in the service, right?" Anita said.

I nodded.

"Did you see any combat?"

"Where are we headed?" I stared out the window. A few drops of rain splattered on the glass.

"My house. In Plano."

I sighed. "Start at the beginning."

CHAPTER THIRTEEN

The Professor parked the stolen Ford with the corpse in the trunk in front of Plano City Hall, a four-story monolithic building located on Avenue K, near the older downtown section of the otherwise shiny and new suburban city. The relatively new government structure seemed out of place with the kitschy storefronts and cobblestone streets of the touristy downtown area.

While driving north after leaving his now-compromised safe house in Dallas, he'd debated moving the hastily hidden body of the contractor to a more secure place. In the end, he'd decided the risk of a second disposal outweighed the risk of discovery by the authorities.

He stepped out of the car and pulled on a tweed sport coat before walking through the front doors and into the foyer of the city building. The entry chamber was open and well lit, with marble floors and pale walls. Along one side of the room was a row of black-and-white photographs, images of stern-faced Caucasian men looking stonily into the camera. He walked closer and saw that they were the mayors of Plano, presented chronologically.

In the middle of the room was a large round counter, like a kiosk, behind which sat a young African American woman wearing a telephone headset. He approached her with his most disarming smile. "Where can I find the department that handles building permits?"

"Go down there." The woman pointed to a hallway by the front entrance. "Last door on your left."

The Professor thanked her. A few moments later he pushed open a glass door marked PLANNING AND ZONING/BUILDING PERMITS and entered a large office zigzagged with cubicles.

He asked a dull-eyed young man behind the front desk about building permits.

"What do you want to know?" The man spat a mouthful of brown saliva into a small Styrofoam cup.

The Professor tried to suppress his nausea. "I need to check on the permits for a house that is under construction."

"Gimme the address." The man flipped a piece of paper on the desk, dropping a pencil on top.

The Professor wrote down the information.

The man tapped on a keyboard for a few minutes. "Construction's been halted. Looks like no insurance for the contractor."

"So no one has been working on the site?"

"Nope." The man shook his head. "Not legally anyway."

"Could you give me the name of the contractor and the owner?"

"Sure." The man spat into the cup again before scribbling a few lines of text on the piece of paper. "That all you need?"

"Yes, thank you." The Professor picked up the paper and headed toward the door.

"Hey, mister," the man said.

The Professor turned around.

"Where'd you get those shades? They're cool."

The Professor touched the designer frames on his temples. The lenses were lightly mirrored, appearing to be clear but not so. He had noted a similar style recently, worn by a young male country-and-western singer of ambiguous sexual orientation.

"I, uh, bought them at the mall."

"Which one?"

"You wouldn't know it." The Professor smiled. "It's in another place."

Anita Nazari lived on a street of dreams, a serene strip of concrete near the pinnacle of the American nirvana. Carefully manicured lawns surrounded shiny new houses in the suburbs, far from the troubles of the inner city.

But not far enough.

She pulled to the curb in front of her home and stopped the car when it was even with the slate sidewalk leading to the house. She got out. I did the same.

"Nice place," I said. The stucco had been painted a lemon yellow. The front porch was covered by a two-story archway, the curve at the top matching the arc of the front windows.

"The school system is good here." Anita walked to the front of the house.

"Where's the jack-in-the-box?"

"There." She pointed to the city-issued garbage can sitting at the end of the driveway by the street. "Actually, it's probably not anymore. They've already picked up the trash."

"You didn't save it?"

"Why on earth would I do such a thing?" Her voice became shrill. "A reminder of the threat to my only child?"

"Oh, I dunno. Evidence, maybe?" When her face paled at my remark, I shrugged and tried to look like it didn't matter.

Anita Nazari closed her eyes and took a deep breath. "If it doesn't interfere with your investigative technique, why don't you come inside?"

I followed her into the house, marveling at the sameness of current residential architecture.

Stairs in the middle of the entryway, next to a hallway leading back.

To the right was a dining room. To the left was a small living room opening onto a wood-paneled library, its shelves all but empty. Between the two rooms was a wet bar.

Lots of expensive molding everywhere. The dining area had padded walls, the fabric a patterned green silk. The floor was dark hardwood, roughly finished to look like it belonged in a peasant farmhouse and not a million-dollar suburban home.

I imagined what the back half would look like. A vast open area, family room on one side, designer kitchen on the other.

Without speaking, Anita walked down the hallway.

I followed her into a vast open area, family room on one side, designer kitchen on the other. The rear of the house overlooked a covered brick patio with a built-in grill. Beyond that was a swimming pool.

"I simply must have the name of your decorator." I strolled around the family room and checked out the fifty-inch LCD screen hanging over the stone fireplace, trying to suppress my envy.

I tend to be realistic. I don't lust after much that I can't have: Angelina Jolie. Another Super Bowl appearance for the Cowboys. And a soft-as-butter La-Z-Boy recliner in front of a hi-def television. Is any of that too much to ask? Well, maybe the Cowboys part.

"I worked hard to be where I am," she said. "I am not about to lose it."

"Did you save the last e-mail?"

She nodded and sat down beside a laptop resting on the kitchen counter. After tapping a few keys, she motioned for me to join her.

I sat on the bar stool next to hers and read the messages. It was from a Hotmail account, the user name a nonsensical series of numbers and letters.

"Address have any significance?"

"No."

I looked at the headers and saw nothing unusual. Then again, I could barely spell RAM, so that didn't mean much.

"You were in the front yard, right?"

"Yes."

"Let's go outside and you show me how it happened."

"Would you like a drink? Or something to eat?"

"No."

"I could make some tea."

I shook my head and walked toward the front door.

"It's no trouble . . ." Her voice trailed off as I reached the entrance.

I stepped outside and looked up and down the block. The houses were all new—and big. I doubted if any was smaller than four bed-rooms, maybe four or five thousand square feet.

Anita Nazari stood beside me on the porch.

"I was there." She pointed to the flower bed. "Tom drove up."

"Tom?"

"A man I've been seeing for the past couple of months." She waved her hand in a dismissive gesture. "He's unimportant."

"Poor Tom." I smiled for a moment.

"Are you *mocking* me?"

"It was a joke."

She didn't reply.

"Never mind." I quit smiling. "Tell me what happened."

"I told her to go inside." Anita hugged herself. "But she went to the curb. The blast was so loud."

"Did anybody call the police?"

"What are you talking about?"

Conversing with Dr. Anita Nazari was an interesting exercise. I asked about apples. She responded with an incomprehensible comment on Paraguayan fruit flies.

"About the explosion," I said. "Did you call the police? Did any of your neighbors hear it?"

"No." She pursed her lips. "It seemed louder to me than it was."

"Tell me about your neighbors." I headed toward the curb and the trash can.

"I don't know them all that well." Anita followed. "A lawyer and his family live across the street. They have a son a year older than Mira. Oh, and Tom, he lives behind me."

I looked in the trash can. It was empty except for a brownish sludge in one corner that smelled like rotten cantaloupe. The receptacle stood next to the brick mailbox, which was resting on a concrete pad by the entrance to the driveway. I leaned against the mailbox and put my eyes level with the top, peering down the street. All the other mailboxes were the same height, set in exactly the same place on their respective lots. Things were certainly orderly and regimented in the suburbs.

"Do you know anything about the people who own the house under construction?" I pointed to a half-finished home across the street and down a couple of lots.

"No."

"That would be the ideal place." I drummed my fingers on the top of the mailbox. "A clear line of sight to your front yard."

"What are you going to do?" Anita Nazari said.

"Investigate."

"I thought you were out of the business." Her tone was sarcastic.

I ignored her and walked down the street.

CHAPTER FOURTEEN

The Professor turned on the scanner and listened for any police chatter. Nothing appeared to be going on except the usual suburban law enforcement issues of a typical Monday. Stray dogs, illegally parked cars, busybody neighbors. No mention of a man wanted in connection with a murder at a construction site or a body found in the neighborhood.

This gave him pause. Why hadn't the witness notified the authorities? Maybe he didn't want to get the police involved for reasons of his own. The Professor smiled for just a moment before shutting off the machine.

He put on a windbreaker and a tie, grabbed a clipboard, and got out of the car, heading for the alley running behind the house where he'd hidden yesterday. He knew his actions were well outside the scope of work for this assignment. He was returning to the scene, and he'd been specifically warned against doing so by his employer.

But he had no choice.

The alley was immaculate, not so much as a soft drink can lying around. The Professor held the clipboard in one hand and feigned interest in the power lines running behind the houses. He walked toward the home where he'd hidden the day before, jotting notes as he went. The air was fresh and clean, the nearest highway and its mass of petro-chemical pollutants miles away.

The Professor felt good. He felt alive. He was on the move again, doing what he did best.

He heard tires crunch on the pavement behind him. He turned around, then smiled and nodded before resuming his investigation of the power lines.

The police car drove slowly by him and turned into the driveway of the house under construction.

I walked down Anita Nazari's street toward the half-built house. The exterior was raw, nothing but Tyvek panels on the outside, making it hard to tell what the finished product was going to look like.

The place next door, nearest to Anita's, had three stories and was constructed to look like a British manor. The English country house effect might have worked a little better if the yard had grass installed. Or even trees. The one on the other side looked like something Liberace might have designed if he'd been an architect.

I walked inside through the gap where a front door would go. The interior was silent, no workers anywhere that I could tell.

The raw design felt similar to Anita's: stairs in the middle of the entryway, a hallway leading to the back where the granite countertops and stainless designer appliances would go.

I headed up to the second floor and went to the front, where the house faced the street. In one of the bedrooms I found what appeared to be a table assembled from discarded chunks of construction material. The makeshift piece of furniture sat at an angle to the rest of the room, about four feet away from the window opening.

It could have been built as a sawhorse, but I doubted it.

I stood behind the table, my thighs pressed against the edge of the wood so that I was facing the same way it was aligned.

I looked out the window. The positioning provided a perfect view of Anita Nazari's front yard. A couple of cinder blocks were lying to one side of the platform, next to a piece of three-quarter-inch plywood. I put the blocks behind the table and placed the wood across them, forming a stool about the right height for an adult to sit on in relation to the table.

I sat down. Propped my arms up as if I were holding a rifle.

"Bang." I squeezed an imaginary trigger. The setup was perfect for surveillance—or a hit. The target would have been about seventy or eighty yards away, an easy shot with a silenced rifle. Or well within range of a remote control device.

I stood up.

The piece of plywood slid off the cinder blocks, hitting the floor with a thud.

Footsteps downstairs. A voice on a radio squawked once before being silenced in midsentence.

My choices were limited. Out the window or down the half-finished steps. I chose the latter and walked down the stairs and into the hallway.

The Plano police officer was young, maybe twenty-five. He was a weight lifter, chest the size of a beer keg. He held a semiautomatic pistol in the prescribed two-handed grip, pointing it at my heart.

"Freeze," the cop said.

"Hi, how're you doing?" I placed my hands on top of my head.

A man in his midforties appeared behind him. He was expensively dressed in a pair of starched khakis, alligator loafers, and a golf shirt. He had a gold bracelet around each wrist, a Presidential Rolex on the left one.

"Who the hell are you?" he said.

"Nobody important." I smiled.

"I own this house."

"Good for you."

"Okay, smart guy." The cop holstered his piece and shoved me against the wall. "Assume the position."

I did as requested and ran the numbers in my head. Back in the life for about an hour and cuffed already.

The cop patted me down, pulled out my wallet, and left me leaning against the unfinished drywall. He removed my ID.

"Says your name is . . . Lee Oswald?"

"Yep."

"Let me see that." Mr. Homeowner grabbed the driver's license. "What are you doing up here? You live in Dallas." He said the last part with a trace of condescension.

"Just passing through."

"Don't know how it is in Big D." The cop slapped one side of a set of handcuffs on my right wrist. "But here in Plano, we've got laws against trespassing."

"There's no door," I said. "Or signs."

The cop pulled my arms behind me and snapped the other end of the cuffs in place without saying anything.

"Bring him into the kitchen." Mr. Homeowner's tone sounded like he was used to giving orders.

"You in charge or is he?" I spoke to the cop as he guided me toward the rear of the house.

The police officer didn't respond. He tightened his grip on my elbow until it hurt.

We entered the kitchen area. No drywall installed yet, only studs, fiberglass insulation, and plastic PVC pipes jutting up from the floor like perfectly round stalagmites.

The homeowner was standing by the rear wall. The cop pushed me that way. After a few more feet he stopped and pointed to the ground. "You know anything about that, Mr. Lee Oswald?"

A large brown stain about two feet square was on the plywood sub-flooring. It looked like someone had tried to mop it up but the porous nature of the wood made the job impossible. Several flies buzzed around the perimeter of the stain.

"That's blood," the homeowner said.

I raised an eyebrow. "That's one opinion."

"I don't think I like your attitude very much." He shook one wrist; his bracelet and watch rattled.

"Mr. Jenkins has had some problems with the construction of his home." The cop pointed to the homeowner. "Contractor went flaky on him."

"What's that got to do with me?"

The cop shrugged. "We've got what looks like a bloodstain and you trespassing."

"This place is an attractive nuisance." I nodded toward the front. "No doors anywhere."

"What are you? A lawyer?" Jenkins put his hands on his hips.

I looked at the cop. "You gonna charge me with anything?"

He pulled a radio from his belt and recited my name and driver's license number into the mouthpiece.

Footsteps sounded from the front of the house. The three of us turned as a middle-aged man wearing thick glasses, chinos, and a cheap-looking blazer entered the room. He had an ID tag clipped to his breast pocket.

"What's going on in here?" he said.

"Who the hell are you?" Jenkins puffed up, thumbs hitched in his belt.

"Building inspector." The man cocked his head to one side. "Who the hell are *you*?"

"Uhhh." Jenkins's face turned pale.

"Somebody called in a bunch of work going on here over the weekend," the new man said. "On a closed site."

"That's impossible." Jenkins had recovered a little bit. "I certainly haven't hired anybody."

The inspector looked around the room for a few moments and then spoke to the cop. "You okay if I nose around a little?"

"Fine with me." The officer put his radio back on his belt and pointed to Jenkins. "Property owner reported a possible crime scene. Let me fill you in." He motioned to the front of the house. Both city officials walked that way.

Jenkins licked his lips a few times and watched them go. When they were out of earshot he said, "You better tell me what's going on here."

"Did you hire somebody to work here while the contractor situation got straightened out?"

He didn't say anything. The air was getting hotter. Beads of perspiration dotted his forehead.

"Maybe somebody who's not too picky about green tags and pulling permits?"

"I've got payments on two houses," he said. "You have any idea what this contractor flap is costing me?"

"Who did you hire?" I took a step closer and kept my voice low.

"My brother-in-law said they were good." He leaned against a sawhorse. "And cheap."

The cop's radio buzzed from the front of the house. The inspector said something I couldn't understand. The noise sounded close.

"How about a name?"

"That's really blood, isn't it?" Jenkins pointed to the stain, a confused look on his face now.

I nodded. "Probably so."

The cop laughed once. Footsteps headed our way.

"How do I know you didn't kill someone here?" Jenkins said.

"You don't." I shrugged as best I could with the handcuffs on. "But if you don't tell the cop to cut me loose, I'm going to tell the inspector you hired me to work here illegally."

He opened his mouth but didn't say anything.

The two city officials returned.

"What about this guy?" The cop pointed to me. "He's clean."

Jenkins shook his head slowly. "Let him go."

The officer undid my handcuffs. I headed to the front door as the inspector started writing on his clipboard.

CHAPTER FIFTEEN

The Professor got back into the stolen Ford and stared at the clipboard, contemplating his next move.

The gullibility of the general population never ceased to amaze him. That he could act like a minor bureaucrat in an insignificant city in this godforsaken state. That he could bluff cooperation from a self-important toad such as Jenkins. That an actual police officer would fail to see through the charade.

His acting skills aside, however, the cleanup plan was not progressing satisfactorily.

A visit to the city offices as well as to the house where he had encountered the contractors had yielded little new information. After checking in with his employer, he would have to head west and search for the missing man, using the address on the card as a starting point. He would have about twenty-four hours to find and eliminate the witness before having to contact his employer again.

Before he left, though, he wanted to learn what he could about the hard-eyed man with the improbable name.

Lee Oswald.

The property owner appeared eager to have Oswald leave as soon as possible, even though he'd been detained for trespassing. The Professor wanted him to stick around, cuffed preferably, until he could determine what if any part the man played in the messy little drama that was the life of Anita Nazari, but to insist could have called attention to himself and his forged City of Plano ID. So he let the man wander away, without so much as a peek at which direction he went.

The Professor started the car with the intention of driving toward a nearby Starbucks and the anonymous Internet connection it offered. Before he could put the transmission into gear, an idea popped into his head.

The most likely scenario was that Oswald worked for the Opposition. He was fit and carried himself like a player in the game, a man accustomed to living on the fringes of society.

On the other hand, there was something about the way he talked, the insolence in the few words the Professor had overheard him speak before entering the kitchen. Most operatives would have remained quiet, offering only minimal comments.

Not this Oswald fellow.

Could he be working for someone other than the Opposition?

The Professor switched off the ignition and got back out of the car, clipboard in hand.

I pushed open Anita Nazari's front door without knocking. A blast of cold air carrying the cloying smell of men's aftershave hit me in the face.

I recognized the cologne.

Brut. The musky scent worn by the make-out artists of my youth, the boys who would be men, teenage Lotharios in Izods and Top-Siders, trolling through the Reagan-era shopping malls of Dallas in search of Laura Ashley–wearing young women.

A man about my age stood by the stairs. He was heavyset, like a linebacker after too much beer and pizza, and wore a two-button gray suit that was just a tad too tight, a white oxford cloth shirt with a striped tie, and a slightly confused look on his face.

I said, "Hi."

"You just open the door to a lady's house and stroll on in?"

"Uh, I've already been here." I pointed to the back. "Anita and I were in the kitchen just a few minutes ago."

"Ahh-nee-ta?" He crossed his arms, pronouncing each syllable.

"Then I went outside, see, and I was across the street and . . ." My voice trailed off. I figured him to be the boyfriend who was deemed "unimportant." I was starting to understand what she meant.

The man frowned.

"I'm Hank Oswald." I scratched my chin for a moment, trying to come up with something reasonable. "Anita's security consultant."

"Security?" He knitted his brow, the wheels turning somewhere in there.

"Yeah." I smiled and wondered where my newest client was at the moment. "Trying to make sure everything is safe."

"Safe?"

"Actually, this really isn't my kind of gig," I said. "I used to be a private investigator."

"Investigator?"

I sighed and slumped my shoulders "Moose, you and I are never going to get anywhere if you keep repeating everything I say." I walked around him toward the kitchen.

The man followed.

Anita Nazari was by the sink, talking on her cell phone. She hung up and raised an eyebrow at me. "What did you learn?"

I sat down at the counter but didn't say anything. Moose entered the room. I looked at him. He looked at me. We both turned to Anita.

She pointed to the man. "This is Tom."

"Hi, Tom."

"Anita, what's going on?" He waved his hands. "Who is this guy?"

"I'm worried about my safety." She sat down by the laptop. "*Apparently,* I need to hire someone to share my concern."

"Are you taking drugs?" Tom said.

"*What?*" Anita frowned.

"I saw a story on *20/20* about doctors prescribing themselves stuff."

"Why don't you just leave?" Anita said.

"I came over to apologize. For yesterday."

Anita nodded.

"You're sure you're not popping pills?" Tom said.

"*No.*"

I sighed and looked at my watch.

"I'll be around, Anita." Tom glared at me. "If you need anything." He exited by the back door.

"See you later." I waved at the door.

"I'm sorry," Anita said.

"Don't worry about it." I shrugged. "Me and boyfriends have never gotten along."

"He's not my boyfriend."

"Gotcha."

"You are infuriating."

I nodded.

Anita took several deep breaths before speaking again. "What did you learn at the house across the street?"

I explained about the bloodstain, the illegal contractors, and the owner's nervousness when the building inspector arrived. I played down the police part.

"You were arrested?" Her mouth gaped open.

"More like detained for a moment."

"You didn't tell them about me, did you?"

I shook my head as the sounds of a sitcom laugh track drifted down the back stairs.

Anita looked at the ceiling and shook her head. "She's supposed to be doing her homework."

"Kids today. When I was her age, we only had basic cable."

"Are you always this sarcastic?"

"Only on days that end in *y*."

Anita cupped her mouth with one hand and yelled at the stairs. *"Mira."*

A few moments later a girl on the brink of puberty clomped her way down the steps wearing oversized sneakers that made her already bird-thin legs look skinnier. She looked like she was going to speak but stopped when she saw me standing there.

"Mira, this is my . . . friend, Mr. Oswald."

"Hi," the girl said.

"Hey, nice to meet you." I grinned.

"You have things to do other than watch television," Anita said.

"Are you and my mom, like, hooking up?" Mira resembled her mother, thick dark hair, a prominent nose, high cheekbones.

I stifled a laugh.

"The term is dating, as we've discussed before, and no, Hank, er, Mr. Oswald and I are not." Anita sighed. "He is an employee, doing some work for me."

"What kind of work?" Mira frowned.

"I'm like the yard guy but I don't sweat as much," I said.

"You're funny." Mira giggled.

Anita shook her head, clearly annoyed. "Mr. Oswald is checking on our security. We talked about how important that is before, remember?"

"Oswald's the name of the guy that shot the president, isn't it?" Mira looked at me and then at her mother.

"If you believe the Warren Commission," I said. "Don't worry; I'm not related to Lee Harvey."

"That's good." Mira smiled. "I feel safer already."

We both laughed.

"Don't you have homework and chores?" Anita said.

Mira, still giggling a little, grabbed a purple knapsack from the floor and plopped it onto the kitchen table.

Anita turned to me. "Now, what is your plan?"

I didn't reply. Therein lay the problem. I wanted nothing more than to find an out-of-the-way bar where I could sling drinks a few hours each week. I wanted to tell lies to naive flight attendants in order to sleep with them. I wanted to do anything other than the occupation for which I was most suited.

What I didn't want to do was to continue to investigate Anita Nazari's strange threats or to track down Mike Baxter's missing daughter.

I rubbed my eyes and said, "I'll need to borrow a car."

CHAPTER SIXTEEN

The Professor sauntered down the alley behind Anita Nazari's block. He kept the clipboard in one hand, a pen in the other, as he pretended to inspect the rear of the homes on either side.

Each house had a wooden privacy fence protecting the backyard. The fences ran about three-quarters of the width of each lot before cutting in to allow the driveways to have access to the rear-entry garages. More than a few of the garages were open, displaying tiny vignettes from the canvas of suburban life.

Women in track suits buckling up toddlers in car seats.

Maids taking out the garbage.

The occasional husband coming home early from work, dressed in the corporate uniform of the day, slacks and a golf shirt.

The sheer material wealth displayed in the *storage* area of a typical suburban home fascinated him. Expensive motorcycles, outdated but still new electronic equipment, shiny sports cars, athletic gear, and enough tools and scrap material to build an office tower.

In the middle of the block, a woman in a terry-cloth robe kissed a man in front of a Mercedes parked at an angle in the driveway. They were both in their late thirties, the picture of health and prosperity and all the good things this country had to offer to the upper middle class: bulging retirement accounts, steady jobs, plenty of material wealth, and a safe neighborhood in which to enjoy it all.

They jumped apart when he walked by, and the Professor wondered where their respective spouses were at the moment.

At the end of the block, on the corner, was Anita Nazari's behemoth of a house.

The Professor stopped and pulled out his clipboard, pretending to take notes regarding the status of her privacy fence.

The rear gate opened.

The Professor reached underneath his jacket for the Ruger.

A young girl, maybe ten or eleven, stepped into the alley, carrying a brown grocery sack. She had a music player fastened to the waistband of her shorts, the white earpieces in place.

The Professor felt his spine stiffen as he realized who the child was.

Mira, Anita Nazari's offspring.

He tried not to stare, concentrating on his clipboard instead.

"Hi." The girl placed the sack on the pavement.

"Hello." The Professor scribbled gibberish on a piece of scratch paper.

"What are you doing?" She pulled the earpieces out.

"I'm with the city." He lowered the clipboard and smiled. The girl was a miniature version of her mother, long limbs, angular face, olive skin.

"Why are you looking at our house?" The girl picked up the sack and hugged it to her chest.

"I'm looking at all the houses on this block, not just yours." He willed himself to be professional even as he thought of what would become of this girl. Children shouldn't have to pay for the sins of their parents.

Mira didn't respond. She carried the sack to a green plastic canister about four feet in diameter and maybe a meter tall.

The Professor pointed to the object. "What's that?"

"It's a composter." Mira dumped the contents of the paper sack inside. "My mom and me are making compost for the yard. It's organic."

"Doing things the organic way is good." The Professor stuck the clipboard under one arm as if his work were finished.

The girl stared at him for a few moments before speaking again. "You're the building inspector, aren't you?"

"Yes." The Professor forced a smile. An unusual term for a young girl to come up with so easily. "How did you know that?"

"My mom's new friend, Hank, he told my mom that the building inspector was down the street."

"Hank is your mother's boyfriend?" The Professor asked, wondering how far he could push.

"Oh, no. He works for my mom on account of she likes to have people around so she can tell them what to do."

"Well, then it's a good thing she's got Mr. . . . ." The Professor raised an eyebrow.

"Oswald." The girl nodded thoughtfully. "Like the man that killed Kennedy."

"Mr. Oswald. Hank Oswald," the Professor said. "It's good that he's—"

"We went to the Sixth Floor Museum this semester," Mira interrupted him. "It's in Dallas, where they have the window where the real Oswald shot the president from."

The Professor nodded, torn between listening to the girl's ramblings and processing the information that Anita Nazari had actually hired someone such as Oswald.

"And my friend Suzy, she, like, totally has this crush on this guy named Ben and they so got busted in a closet, like, totally making out."

"Bad news for Suzy, right?" He stuck his ballpoint pen into his breast pocket.

"Why do you wear those funny sunglasses?"

"The, uh, light bothers me." The Professor touched the frames of his shades instinctively, nonplussed at her verbal curveball.

"Hank doesn't wear sunglasses."

"What job does . . . Hank do for your mother?" He regretted the question as soon as the words left his lips.

Mira frowned and crossed her arms. A jet spewed a thick contrail on the far horizon as a Suburban sped down the cross street a few dozen feet from the back of Anita Nazari's home. A few awkward seconds passed.

"I must be going. Other houses to inspect." The Professor tapped his clipboard. Rule One of covert operations: If you suspect your cover is blown, get out as soon as possible. He walked toward the cross street.

Mira inched backward to the gate. "Mama hired him to make her feel safe."

"Feel safe?" The Professor stopped. "Sounds like she should call the police."

"No." The girl's voice was soft. "Mama would never do that."

"I could call the police for you, if that would help."

Mira shook her head. "Hank will take care of things. He's tough, I can tell."

"What is it that makes your mother feel unsafe?" Another less than discreet question, but at this point, what did it matter?

No response.

"Is there anything I can do?" He smiled.

"I-I-I have to go. I need to finish my homework." She opened the gate but kept looking at him. A second later, she was gone.

The Professor stared at the fence around Anita Nazari's house. Although new, it was wooden and flimsy and provided no real protection save from prying eyes.

"Safe?" he said. "No one is ever safe."

He turned and walked back down the alley.

CHAPTER SEVENTEEN

I slammed the door of the lime green Volkswagen Bug. A perfectly nice Range Rover sat by the curb. Anita Nazari's *second* car, the one she bought on a whim for her fortieth birthday, had white leather seats, a lollipop-shaped air freshener hanging from the rearview mirror, and an oversized flower sticker on the back window.

Beggars, choosers, and all that other stuff.

I cranked on the ignition. The speakers blared out 1980s Madonna before I slapped the OFF button. I pulled out of the meticulously kept garage and backed down the driveway, waving at Anita standing by the back door of her suburban castle with the metaphorically leaky moat.

I drove out of the alley and then down the street past the house under construction. No activity was visible. The homeowner and two city officials appeared to be gone.

At the cross street, I put the transmission into park and evaluated what I knew.

Somebody was threatening Anita Nazari on an ongoing basis.

The latest incident was yesterday, a fairly sophisticated action requiring planning and surveillance.

The best place to coordinate the action was the house under construction.

The amount of blood at that location indicated that someone had either been severely wounded or had died there, more probably the latter. Logically, that meant either the instigator of the attacks or another interested party.

Since the operation appeared to be the work of a professional, logic again dictated he or she was not the victim. Which meant the other party was. Which meant there was a body somewhere yet to be discovered by the authorities, or I wouldn't have been cut loose.

The question now was whether the instigator of the attacks had enough easily accessible resources to properly dispose of the body. If yes, then a search would be futile. That was the only avenue open to me at the moment, though, so I decided to proceed as if the attacker had been operating in haste.

I drummed my fingers on the steering wheel of the VW and tried to figure the best place to stash a body in the suburbs.

Back in the day, I knew a guy who knew a guy who could make a corpse disappear for two grand, no questions asked, so long as you delivered the stiff to the right place, usually a block or two from one of the government housing construction sites in West Dallas. The fact that I could remember the name of the first guy, and what bar to find him in, bothered me more than a little.

I put the car in gear and drove off, looking for construction sites.

Before the postwar population explosion, Plano had been a farming community, a minor stop for the trains headed north from the bustling metropolis of Dallas. In the sixties, Dallas, a city with no real reason to exist other than the dogged determination of a handful of pioneers, began to grow exponentially, gobbling up more and more blackland prairie.

The result was a huge amount of construction needed to feed the explosion of human beings, an ever-growing splotch on the map like the zombie virus in some bad sci-fi movie. Dots blossomed here and there as existing towns succumbed to the people plague, followed quickly by a flood in the empty areas that used to grow corn and sorghum.

Anita's street was one of the northernmost in that particular subdivision. I drove clockwise, in widening circles, looking for a likely spot.

To the south and west lay a developer's demented vision of Western European architecture, street after street of mammoth new homes on tiny lots, built to resemble English castles or French châteaus with the occasional Italian villa thrown in for a little Mediterranean flavor.

A few blocks east, across Coit Road, was an older development with a real neighborhood feel to it, the houses modest but much more appealing with mature trees lining the streets and children's toys lying about in most of the front yards.

Six blocks north, Anita's subdivision stopped abruptly, replaced by flat pastureland stretching to the horizon, dotted by the occasional scrawny post oak. I imagined I could see the Oklahoma border in the distance.

The boundary was on an old farm-to-market road that was under construction, apparently being widened. The street leading from Anita's subdivision dipped, and the Volkswagen rattled over the temporary asphalt.

On the far side lay a series of concrete pipes, each maybe thirty feet long and ten in diameter, resting in front of a long ditch running the length of the road as far as I could see in either direction. New sewer lines to contain the tons of wastewater generated by the new subdivisions.

I maneuvered across the road and stopped on the shoulder. This far north, the traffic was minimal, an occasional pickup every minute or so.

I got out and locked the VW. The air smelled like fresh-turned earth and fertilizer. The sky was cloudless but hazy, the color of faded blue jeans that needed a wash. A thunderstorm was visible far to the south, probably over downtown Dallas. Within a few moments, sweat dribbled down the small of my back.

I approached the first pipe. Weeds grew tall along the curve resting on the ground. There was a gap of about three feet between sections.

I stepped into the space between the nearest two pipes and looked each way. To the left, about a hundred yards away, a small obstruction lay on the bottom, like a lumpy sack of something. The something was too far away to determine what it was.

I got back in the VW and drove west, counting until five pipe sections had passed.

I exited the car again. Stuck my head in the nearest tube. Waved away a cloud of flies, disturbing the heavy odor of spoiled meat wafting in the still air.

The lump was a body, laying facedown.

I took a deep breath, held it, and dashed inside. I flipped the corpse over, disturbing a mass of flies.

The man's face was gray like the concrete upon which it rested, his midsection swollen with the gases of decomposition. His mouth was closed in a tight little grimace, in sharp contrast to the ragged cut where his throat should have been. He wore jeans, heavy work boots, and an old U2 concert T-shirt. Popmart 1998.

I suppressed my gag reflex as much as possible and felt his pockets. Nothing in three out of the four, not so much as a penknife or a lighter. In the rear right, I found a wallet. I pulled it out. Opened it. Three twenty-dollar bills, two fives, and a one. No ID, no credit cards, no insurance info.

I ran out of the tube gasping for air and heaved in a couple of lungfuls, sweat pouring down my face. A flatbed truck carrying stacks of Sheetrock lumbered by on the farm-to-market road; otherwise no sound disturbed the hot afternoon.

I examined the wallet in the sunlight. It was worn and sweat stained, much like you'd expect after residing in the back pocket of a construction worker. I looked in each crevice several times before tossing it on the ground.

I said, "Crap."

Nobody heard me but the flies.

I dashed back inside the tube and started over, this time pulling off the man's work boots and finding nothing but dirty socks, before sticking my hands all the way into his pockets.

The flies were not happy.

Again nothing, except a wad of lint in the left rear, which I removed because I wanted something to show for my effort.

With my stomach lurching and sweat stinging my eyes, I again stumbled out of the rank concrete tube and went to the shady side, out of sight from the road.

I sat down and looked at the wad of material clutched in my hand. It wasn't lint. I worked it apart and saw it was a business card that had been through the laundry. It had been folded over a couple of times. A name and number were written on the back in barely legible lettering.

Roxanne or Roseanne. The letters were all but indecipherable. The numbers were worse. Eight, one, and that was it. The funny part was that the washing hadn't made them unreadable; the penmanship had. I recognized the cryptic message for what it probably was: a drunken barroom notation to call Roxanne or Roseanne or whoever.

I flipped the card over and found what I wanted.

Name: Patrick Toogoode.

Address: Camp Bowie Boulevard, Fort Worth, Texas.

Occupation: Roofing and general contractor.

And the best part, a hint that there might be a another witness out there.

Name of the Company: Toogoode and Toogoode, Contractors. Brothers working together since 1997.

I smiled and walked back to the VW.

CHAPTER EIGHTEEN

I pulled into Anita Nazari's driveway and got out. Even though it was late in the afternoon and very hot for the time of the year, the street was active.

Children on bikes. Suburbans and minivans slowly going by. Attractive thirtyish women pushing strollers and walking golden retrievers.

I nodded hello to an elderly couple in matching baby blue running suits as they power-walked down the street, elbows a blur pistoning in time with their steps.

Anita opened the door before I got across the lawn. She didn't say anything, motioned for me to enter.

"Hi, honey, I'm home."

She frowned. "What?"

"How was the Beaver today?" I stepped inside. "Did that little scamp do his homework?"

She shut the door, a confused look on her face.

"How about a beer? Been a long day." I hadn't had a drink in a month or more. I added another tally to the mental score sheet: Back in the life an hour? In handcuffs. A half day as a PI? Drinking again.

She wrinkled her nose. "You smell."

"It's dirty work, this private investigating."

I followed her into the kitchen.

Mira sat at the kitchen counter, a notebook open, pencil between her teeth. She looked at me and smiled.

Anita stood behind her, one hand on the girl's shoulder in a distinctly protective manner.

Mira coughed, a deep bronchial-sounding eruption. When she stopped, her breath was a wheeze.

"When did this start?" Anita said.

"It's nothing, Mom." The girl bent over her notebook.

"Allergies getting to you?" I smiled.

Mira smiled back and coughed. "It was a red ozone day."

"Go wash up." Anita rubbed her eyes. "We're having an early dinner."

Mira stood up.

Anita placed her palm on the girl's head. "Use your inhaler."

"I'll be okay." Her daughter headed for the back stairway.

Neither of us spoke until Mira was gone. Then Anita said, "She is not well."

"She looks healthy."

"Her immune system is compromised. Environmental pollutants make it worse." Anita waved a hand at nothing. "I wouldn't expect you to understand."

"Try me. I'm not as dumb as I look."

"What did you learn?" Anita went to the refrigerator and got out a bottle of white wine and a beer.

"Maybe nothing. Maybe everything."

She was in midpour with the wine but stopped.

I took the beer and opened it. "I'm going to Fort Worth tomorrow, see if I can track down a guy. Can I take the Range Rover?"

"No."

"Fair enough."

"Do I want or need to know the details about what you are doing?"

I shook my head. Anita Nazari was more street smart than she let on.

"Feel free to take the Volkswagen, then."

"Okay." I drank some beer, a Bass Ale. It went down smoothly, like an old, much-missed friend.

"My baby girl." Anita seemed to say the words to herself rather than me. She finished pouring the wine.

I drained the beer and put the empty bottle on the counter. "Do you have a gun?"

She took a drink but didn't say anything. Her eyes were wide, unblinking.

"You might consider getting one." I turned and walked to the front door.

CHAPTER NINETEEN

Before my premature retirement from the investigator gig, I was partners with a sharp-tongued woman named Nolan O'Connor, the niece of my dead mentor.

Nolan was danger personified, a raven-haired, denim-wearing temptress who possessed a beauty usually only seen in the glossy pages of fashion magazines, and a right hook worthy of a Golden Gloves contender.

With a few expert jabs, she could put a three-hundred-pound biker on the floor in a quivering mass and not smudge her lipstick.

She could also drink a Teamster under the table, shatter a beer bottle from across a crowded bar with one bullet, and cause arousal in a sexually ambivalent man twice her age with the arch of an eyebrow. Not long before I'd dropped out, she'd done all three in a single night.

She also had a pool of insecurities deeper than Loch Ness, evidenced by her romantic choices: emotionally retarded, often abusive narcissists close to her own age, or men old enough to be her father.

A month or so after I took my hiatus, Nolan married a seventy-year-old retired venture capitalist named Rufus. They had known each other for a week. She and Rufus lived in a big house near the Dallas Country Club.

Nolan drank too much and tried to fit in with the social scene and swirl of charity parties inherent in her new station in life. She bought expensive clothes from the hoity-toity boutiques in the Highland Park Village, conveniently located only a few blocks away.

She swore she was happy, but don't we all.

I left Anita Nazari's neighborhood and headed toward the Dallas Tollway. As I drove I called Nolan's cell phone. She answered on the fourth ring, her voice shrill and slurred at the same time.

I asked her if I could borrow a computer, Internet access, you know. Needed to do a little research. She said sure thing, c'mon over, and hey, are you back in the biz again? I hung up without answering, put the VW on cruise control, and headed south on the Tollway. Commuters making their way to the suburbs clogged the northbound lanes like rats fleeing a burning ship while traffic the opposite way was blessedly sparse.

I turned on the CD player and sang along with Madonna until my exit.

Rufus had made a bunch of money leveraging this and merging that and had bought himself a large, Spanish-tiled home on a tree-lined street where the acre lots backed up to a serene creek.

I wheeled the Beetle into the circular driveway and got out. The front beds were freshly planted with spring flowers and looked like an impressionistic painting. Two sago palms in planters the size of hot tubs flanked the glass-and-wrought-iron front door.

I rang the bell.

A middle-aged Hispanic woman in a light blue maid's uniform answered the door.

"*Hola,*" I said.

She cocked her head and grimaced at my one-word attempt at Spanish. "Yes?"

"Would you tell Nolan that Hank is here?"

She didn't move.

I smiled.

"*Señora* Nolan?" She raised one eyebrow.

"Yes." I nodded and tried not to look impatient. I'd been to the house several times before and received the same treatment. The staff was very loyal to the one writing the checks.

"*Uno momento.*" She disappeared to the left, where I knew a large study was located.

Thirty seconds later my former partner appeared at the door. She wore a peach and green sundress that stopped about midthigh and several rows of gold and sparkly jewelry on each wrist. Her former wardrobe consisted of faded jeans, a white blouse or T-shirt, and a gun in her back pocket. Times change.

"Heya, Hank."

"Uhh . . . hi." I tried not to look at the tiny pucker on her left leg from a bullet she'd taken during our first time working together, a bone white scar against tan flesh. Instead I stared at her chest, which was at least three cup sizes bigger than the last time I'd seen her.

"Getting an eyeful, huh?" She brushed a few strands of hair behind one ear.

"What the . . . ?"

The maid was standing by the stairs. She made a hissing sound.

"Let's go in there." Nolan pointed to the study.

I followed her into the wood-paneled room. She shut the door behind us and plopped down on a leather sofa by the fireplace.

"They're too big, aren't they?" She cupped a breast in each hand.

I swallowed several times. They were gigantic, as if there were four of us in the room: me, Nolan, and the twins.

"Everybody has them," she said. "It's like you have to. You know, to fit in."

"Right." I stared at her chest. "Fit. In."

"You came to borrow the computer, remember?" She pointed to a large partners' desk by the bay window overlooking a koi pond in the side yard.

"Yeah, thanks." I stood up and blinked. Shook my head a few times.

"You want something to drink?" Nolan went to the wet bar in the corner. "Rufus has got some fancy single malt. Only make like one bottle a year or something like that."

"No, thanks." I sat down behind the desk and tapped the keyboard, erasing the screen saver, a picture of Rufus and Nolan on their wedding day at the Bellagio in Vegas. I double-clicked the Internet Explorer icon as Nolan poured a measure of Skyy Vodka into a highball glass.

I got to Google and entered the name of the contractor.

A couple thousand hits. Several mentions on Craigslist about shoddy work performed on a remodel job. Same mention on a forum devoted to home repairs. No contact information at all. Other than that, nothing relevant in the first few pages.

I tried several variations, using geographical modifiers.

Nada.

Nolan came over and sat on the edge of the desk to the left of the monitor, facing me. She crossed her legs, causing the hem of the already short dress to ride up. She took a sip of her drink.

I returned my attention to the computer. Nolan and I had always existed in an uneasy sexual truce, each keenly aware of the other, only a very thin line keeping us apart.

"Rufus is at the club." She jiggled ice cubes. "It's domino night."

"That so." I typed in the Internet address of a commercial database, one of those find-anybody things. I'd prepaid for a year's worth of searches and still had a few months to go, so I entered my user name (doctorofluv) and password (mother's birthday).

"I might get on the board for the Cattle Baron's Ball."

I stopped typing and looked up. "What on earth for?"

The Cattle Baron's Ball was near the pinnacle of Dallas society. Rich women with nothing but time on their hands vied in a ruthless competition to get on the board. Once there, they spent millions in order to raise thousands for the charity du jour, usually some internal organ in need of repair. Heart, lungs, etc.

I'd gone a couple of years before, at the behest of a very wealthy man who was afraid his latest wife was having an affair. She was. With the man's son. It got really icky in a hurry.

"Why not?" She took a long drink of vodka. "I miss hanging out with you, Hank."

I ignored her and returned my attention to the screen, typing in the name of Mike Baxter's daughter. A few seconds later an address current as of a month ago appeared. I wrote it down before typing in the name of the contractor from the almost disintegrated business card.

"I miss the juice, busting open a case," she said. "Sticking it to the bad guy."

"Not me." I hit ENTER.

"Bull. Lie to your mother, not somebody who knows." She leaned closer, propping herself up on one arm, the movement pulling the material of her dress taut against her new breasts. "You live for it as much as I do. It's what you're good at."

"Whatever." I watched as nothing materialized on the screen except for a hit in North Carolina, a onetime residence for Patrick Toogoode. I tried to figure out what that meant. Very few people were truly invisible, completely off the grid. I tried different spellings. Nothing.

"What are you doing, anyway?" Nolan peered at the screen. "Trying to track somebody down?"

"Yeah."

"So you're working again?"

"No."

"You're lying." She drained her glass and set it down on the desk.

"It's a quick job. Nothing really."

We were both quiet for a few minutes while I tapped. Then Nolan said, "Why didn't you ever take a shot at me?" Her words were definitely slurred now. I wondered how many of those vodkas she'd had before I'd arrived.

"It wouldn't have worked out." I stood up and patted her on the shoulder. "We're the same person. The juice would've burned us out."

"I miss the juice." She looked at me, green eyes welling with tears.

"You mentioned that already." I leaned over the keyboard and for the heck of it entered Anita Nazari's name. The doctor had a long trail, address after address, bouncing around most of the United States, it seemed.

"Let me help you."

I shut down the Web browser. "Women who work as PIs don't get to be on the Cattle Baron's board. I looked it up in the rule book."

"Screw the c-cow women, okay?" She hiccoughed and put one hand on my shoulder. "Take me with you, please. I need to do something other than sit around this place all the time."

I nodded, as if I were pondering the offer. I said, "How is Max?"

She frowned. "What about him?"

Max was Nolan's stepson, Rufus's only offspring. Max was a thirty-two-year-old nerd who lived with his mother. He was also supposed to be a pretty good hacker.

"What's he up to these days?"

She laughed. "He's never had a date in his life and spends all day staring at computer code. I bet he's at home."

"Let's go pay him a visit, then."

CHAPTER TWENTY

I drove. Nolan gave directions.

After a few minutes, she pulled out her cell phone and dialed. From the half of the semicoherent conversation I heard, it appeared she was letting Max know we were coming over. Something about turning off the sensors.

I put the top down on the Beetle. The wind whipped Nolan's hair, and she smiled for the first time that evening. The sun was low in the west, the sky streaked with orange and violet.

I headed west on Lovers Lane toward Dallas Love Field, through the heart of the Park Cities. Small, upscale shops lined either side of the street. A few blocks after Inwood Road the stores became a little dingy. I turned right and headed north. The homes in this area were small, most built right after World War II.

Max lived in a garage apartment behind his mother's house, a few miles west of Rufus's mansion. After a couple more turns I pulled the VW into a narrow driveway underneath a towering live oak. The house was one of the smaller ones on the block, probably a two-bedroom, and the mortar between the bricks had started to fall out. An oscillating sprinkler at the end of a faded green hose fanned water across one half of the lawn.

Nolan dialed her cell phone again. "It's me . . . Yes, we're alone." She looked in my direction.

I nodded.

Nolan hung up. "Max tends to be a little antisocial."

"No fooling?" I got out. "Lead the way."

She slammed the passenger door and walked down the driveway running along the side of the home. The house appeared empty except for the faint blue flickering of a TV through a slit in the drapes.

The structure in the rear was two stories, occupying a corner of the overgrown backyard. The bottom half was a double garage; an outside staircase led to the upper floor.

A late-model Chevy Impala was parked next to a black Nissan Xterra. On the back of the SUV was a bumper sticker that read MY OTHER VEHICLE IS A ROMULAN WARBIRD.

Nolan stopped near the bottom of the stairs. After thirty seconds or so, the upstairs door opened, and Max stepped onto the landing. He wore a gray T-shirt that was a size too small and bell-bottom jeans made to look dirty even when they weren't. His hair was in a ponytail, and he had a scraggly beard on the underside of his chin.

He didn't say anything, just looked at us with a half sneer, half smile plastered on his face.

"Can we come in?" Nolan put one foot on the bottom stair.

Max nodded once.

She walked up. I followed and tried not to stare at her legs underneath the short dress. When we got to the top, the three of us stood in a tight little circle on the landing. Max kept the door shut. He stared at Nolan's chest. Every few seconds he would glance at me and frown before returning his attention to his stepmother.

"So are we going to just stand here?" I said.

Max didn't say anything.

Nolan snapped her fingers.

Max blinked and looked at me, the sneer returning. "Yeah, c'mon in." He opened the door, and we followed him into the upstairs apartment.

The place was one big room, a lot cleaner than I expected. The sleeping area was to the right side, closest to the street. A double bed was in the corner next to a sofa and coffee table. Several posters were tacked on the wall by the bed: *X-Files,* Rage Against the Machine, and a *Lord of the Rings* movie advertisement. A small kitchenette was in the corner. The rest of the place looked like the War Room at the Pentagon.

I stopped counting at eight screens and monitors.

"What do you want?" Max spoke to me but looked at Nolan.

"Is that foil on the windows?" I walked to where glass should have been overlooking the driveway.

"Nolan says you're an investigator."

"Used to be. Now I'm just trying to track somebody down." I picked up a book from the coffee table, a paperback that promised to reveal the secrets of the Illuminati and Freemasons. I put it down next to the latest issue of *Maxim.*

Nolan sat on the couch and closed her eyes.

"If you're not an investigator, then what are you doing looking for people?" Max's tone was accusatory.

"It's a hobby." I smiled and tried to quell my growing irritation.

"My dad says you're a bartender now." He stuck his chest out, going for badass and falling far short of the mark.

Nolan snorted once.

"Max, were you born a punk or did you take lessons?" I wondered what the significance was that my name had come up between father and son.

"You're the one asking for help, jerkface."

I nudged Nolan's foot with mine. "Let's go."

She stood up slowly. Yawned and stretched. Looked at Max and said, "Don't make me tell Daddy you wouldn't help me."

Max scrunched his lips together and blew air through them. He sat down and pulled a wireless keyboard into his lap.

"Can you find somebody who doesn't want to be found?" I smiled, trying to show there were no hard feelings.

Max tilted his head to one side and started talking. Sixty-four-bit this, secure routers that, spoofed IP addresses, UNIX mainframes, blah blah.

"Gotcha." I held up both hands in a gesture of surrender.

Max smirked. "Gimme the info."

"Already Googled and tried a commercial database." I handed him a slip of paper.

"This is gonna take a while."

"How long?" I looked at my watch.

"A day or so." He chewed on his lower lip. "And I'm going to get a buddy to help."

"How much?"

"A thousand."

Nolan shook her head. "I'm calling your father as soon as we get in the car."

"All right, all right." Max stood up and crossed his arms. "How about five hundred?"

"And check out this *client* of his while you're at it." She turned to me. "What was her name?"

I hesitated for a moment, wondering how my former partner knew I had an actual client—and how she knew said client was a female. "Anita Nazari." I spelled it out for him.

Max scribbled the name down on a yellow pad. "That will be an extra hundred."

"Done." I turned and left.

We drove back to Nolan's in silence. The sun had set; traffic was lighter. I pulled into the driveway behind a parked Lexus.

"Looks like Rufus is back." I put the transmission in park. "Domino night must have ended early."

Nolan said, "Are you still living at that flophouse?"

"A Studio Six is hardly a flophouse."

She rolled her eyes as the ornate front door of her new home swung open and a shaft of light swept across the front porch.

"I'll talk to you later." I put the VW in drive.

"I miss you, Hank."

"You're married now and don't need to work anymore."

A figure appeared in the doorway, silhouetted by the light from inside.

"He's twice my age."

"He was when you married him."

"Nolan?" Rufus took a few steps outside. "Is that you?"

"He's got prostate trouble." Nolan lowered her voice even though her husband was too far away to hear. "Gets up at all hours to go to the bathroom."

"What part of 'in sickness and in health' don't you understand?" I drummed my fingers on the wheel, more than a little anxious to avoid playing marriage counselor to a woman I cared for more than I was willing to admit.

She got out. "I'll let you know what Max says."

"Max?" Rufus was by the car now. He wore a double-breasted blazer over a beige silk sweater and linen pants. His thick gray hair was close cropped. He looked like a WASP version of Ralph Lauren.

"Hi, baby." Nolan kissed him on the cheek. "Max was helping Hank check some stuff out. You know, on the computer."

"That so." Rufus looked at me but didn't offer a hand to shake. "Honey, why don't you run on inside while Hank and I visit for a moment? Maybe see what Consuelo's got for dinner?"

I cringed, waiting for the blowup. Nolan once stabbed a man who made a joke about her being barefoot and pregnant in the kitchen.

Nothing happened. My former partner kissed her husband again and scampered away.

Rufus watched her go and then turned to me. He leaned against the car, palms on the top of the door. "Nolan's quite a woman."

I nodded but didn't speak.

"She's got a good life now."

"Rufus—"

"Let me finish." He held up one hand. "What I'm trying to say is I think it would be best if you didn't come around."

I didn't reply.

"One more bit of advice." He leaned in closer, elbows on the door now. He smiled, lips tight across impossibly white teeth. "Stay the hell away from my son."

I shrugged. "Last time I checked, Max is an adult."

"I'm playing in the big leagues." He looked around at his house and the grounds. "You're still trying to figure out how to put on your jock-strap."

CHAPTER TWENTY-ONE

The Professor had always been fascinated by blood.

Life's fluid essence, a sea teeming with trillions and trillions of infinitesimal specks of matter, each perfectly suited to its particular function, whether it was the transportation of oxygen and glucose to fuel the meat carcass or the removal of the waste by-products.

Like any ocean, though, blood also possessed bad elements, tiny dollops of poison lurking beneath the surface, waiting to attack the host.

The Professor knew all too well about toxins in the blood. The doctors had been quite specific about the damage endured after his exposure to certain substances during his last trip to the Gulf.

Fortunately, he wasn't concerned with his own blood at the moment. He forced the memories of the doctors and the sand and the heat from his mind and instead pondered what poisons lurked in the pool of red liquid on the floor underneath where Marty Costello dangled, his arms tied to a hook mounted in the ceiling of the van.

Alcohol definitely. Marty had been drunk when the Professor had found him in the bar on the west side of Fort Worth, intoxicated enough that he had admitted to knowing the Toogoode brothers. The Professor had gotten the name and address of the drinking establishment from the wallet of the man he'd killed.

Marty had been drinking shots of cinnamon-flavored schnapps and mugs of beer. He'd been smoking, too, as had most of the other blue-collar workers, the air in the tavern cloudy with carcinogens.

The Professor sniffed his sleeve and smelled the fumes of burnt tobacco. He imagined the havoc the benzene and carbon monoxide molecules were wreaking on his delicate immune system.

Marty Costello made a noise, trying to speak, probably, a difficult task given the missing teeth and damaged mouth.

The Professor looked at the man and smiled. Marty had told him so much, once the pain had burned through his alcoholic haze. The second contractor, Collin Toogoode, was within his grasp.

He tried to envision Toogoode, what he was doing at that exact moment, if he was eating or drinking or coupling with his wife or girlfriend. The Professor hoped that whatever he was doing, he was enjoying it to the fullest. Because Collin Toogoode's time on earth was drawing to a close.

Marty gurgled. Another few ounces of blood dribbled onto the floor of the panel van.

The Professor pulled out his knife.

CHAPTER TWENTY-TWO

Fort Worth, once the redheaded stepchild a few miles west of the bigger and bolder Dallas, had undergone a metamorphosis in the last decade or so. Where there was once a vagrant-laden downtown, a vibrant city center now thrived, an appealing mix of funky shops, eclectic restaurants, and trendy clubs, all supported by the pedestrians who lived in the nearby high-rise apartments. Big D could take a lesson or three on how to do it right.

I was on Main Street with the top down on the VW, checking out the lunchtime crowds. At a stoplight, I nodded and smiled at a tall brunette wearing a lacy skirt and tight T-shirt that showed a couple of inches of bare midriff. She looked at me, an expression on her face that I hoped was amused detachment but in reality was probably disdain. Must have been the VW.

When the light changed I continued west, past a boot shop on the bottom floor of a five-story brownstone that could have been in Greenwich Village and a restaurant called the Eight-O. A crowd of people dressed in business casual sat on the brick patio of the eating place underneath a canopy of live oaks.

I debated stopping for lunch to see if Emily with the long blond hair and the sunburst tattoo on the small of her back was still a hostess at the restaurant. I decided not to. I had things to do, and Emily was probably still a little miffed since I'd stood her up for her sister's wedding a few months back.

It took me ten minutes to reach the address on the business card, on the far west side of town off Jacksboro Highway, a dingy, four-lane blacktop filled with pawnshops, strip clubs, and used car lots.

I pulled into a parking spot in front of the Emerald Isle Saloon. The bar was in a cinder-block building with blacked-out windows. A neon sign over the door flickered that the establishment was open for business.

The exterior had been painted kelly green sometime during the Ford administration. On one side of the windowless door was a relatively fresh rendition of Bono in a cowboy hat. On the other side was a faded painting of a leprechaun sitting on a longhorn steer.

The Emerald Isle Saloon didn't look like a contractor's place of business. Unfortunately, the address matched the one on the nearly disintegrated card.

I put the top up. Locked the car. Walked inside.

The place was smoky and dark, the tobacco haze lit up by a big-screen TV on one wall and a half-dozen neon beer signs. I blinked a few times to adjust my vision.

An old Willie Nelson song was playing softly on the jukebox. "Whiskey River Take My Mind."

One bartender. Three men sitting at the bar, leaning over mugs of beer. Scattered tables, empty. Conversation stopped as the door shut behind me and everybody turned to look my way.

Without thinking about it, I felt the vacant space on my right hip where the Browning Hi-Power usually resided. I was glad for the Spyderco lockback knife in my belt.

The bartender stuck a cigarette in his mouth and lit it. He blew smoke in my direction but didn't say anything.

I went to the corner of the bar, by a video poker machine, and sat down.

Four sets of eyes sets tracked my movement.

I nodded hello.

Blank stares back. One of the patrons, a tall, skinny guy in a blue work shirt, coughed.

"How about a Guinness?" I pointed to the taps, trying to feel all Irishy.

"The hell are you?" The bartender let a trail of smoke drift from his nostrils.

"I'm Mr. Thirsty." I smiled. "You the bartender?"

He blew a smoke ring at me.

The skinny guy in the blue work shirt pushed himself away from the bar and walked toward me. His shirt had a name tag sewn on it. Ryan Sherlock, of Sherlock Roofing.

He said, "Yuppie bar's on the other side of town."

I was wearing a Pat Green concert T-shirt that had been washed one too many times, faded Wranglers, and a pair of old Justin Roper boots. No jewelry except for a paint-spattered Timex Ironman. I looked about as much like a yuppie as did Michael Jackson.

"I just want a drink." I slapped a ten on the bar.

"Leave him be, Ryan." The bartender placed a glass full of beer the color of motor oil in front of me. The top quarter was straw-colored foam.

"Sorry about that." The bartender scooped up my money. "We had a little trouble in here last night."

"In this place?" I took a sip, getting a foam mustache in the process. "Ce n'est pas possible."

"Huh?" The man stared at me as he put my change down.

"Never mind."

He started to say something else, but a commotion from the other end of the room interrupted him. Ryan Sherlock banged his hand on the bar. The others murmured and shook their heads slowly.

"What happened?" the bartender said.

"Collin's cell phone." Ryan whapped the bar again. "Still no answer."

"Collin?" I said to no one in particular.

"Just who the hell are you?" Ryan took a few steps my way, fists clenched, face flushed. "I told you already the yuppie bar's on the other side of town."

"I'm a friend of Toogoode's." I decided to mix things up a little. "Collin Toogoode."

The bartender sucked in a mouthful of air. The place got quieter, nothing but smoke and Willie's nasal singing filling the room.

Ryan pulled a pistol from his pocket, a black semiautomatic not much bigger than a pack of cigarettes. He spat on the floor and looked at me, one corner of his mouth turned up as if something distasteful were on his tongue.

"Aye, another country folk, asking around." He spoke with a strange accent now, an Irish brogue, but not really. He turned to a man in his early thirties wearing black jeans, a beige silk shirt, and a gold Rolex. "Lock the door, Petey. Let's find out what color this yonk bleeds."

CHAPTER TWENTY-THREE

The Professor pulled off the gravel road that ran through the compound and parked the Ford underneath a live oak tree, a few dozen yards from a small patch of dirt where a woman stood leaning on a hoe. On the other side of the square parcel of earth sat a late-model Cadillac.

She stared at him as he approached.

When he got to the edge of the dirt he saw that the land had been tilled and planted with vegetables. Tomatoes, peppers, and squash grew in neat little rows.

"Hello." He smiled and tried to look as nonthreatening as possible. He wore a pair of khakis and a white T-shirt. The Sig Sauer .40-caliber handgun rested in a holster tucked behind his right hip.

The woman was in her fifties, pale skin, reddish-going-gray hair. She frowned at him but didn't say anything.

"I know that you're a Traveler." He took a few steps in her general direction, between two rows of tomato plants. "I am, too."

She spoke a few words in a language he didn't understand.

"I'm looking for Collin Toogoode." He cut across the row of vegetables. "I have something he needs."

The woman looked at the Cadillac for an instant before returning her gaze to the Professor.

"Perhaps the information is in your car?" The Professor smiled and nodded toward the luxury automobile.

"I don't know what you're talking about," the woman said.

"I mean you no harm."

"The men will be back any minute."

"No, they won't." The Professor shook his head. "Everyone has left like they always do when there's trouble. It's the Traveler way."

The woman tightened her grip on the hoe, knuckles now white.

"But you stayed behind for some reason," he said. "Maybe you don't like to travel as much as the rest of them?"

She swung the hoe, the metal point aimed at his temple.

The Professor had been expecting the attack. He moved a few steps closer and let the wooden shaft connect with the fleshy portion of his forearm. With his other hand he grabbed the hoe and yanked it from her grip.

She took a step backward but not fast enough.

The Professor swung the tool like a baseball bat and hit her on the side of the head, not putting his full strength behind the strike but still using enough force to knock her unconscious for a while and leave a nice goose egg.

She fell to the dirt, landing on top of a pepper plant.

He hoped she wasn't out for a long time, as he might need to interrogate her. He threw the hoe across the gravel road and walked to the Cadillac. The door was unlocked, keys in the ignition. A red leather purse sat in the passenger's seat. He rummaged through its contents and found the information he was seeking in a few minutes.

He would dispatch the woman and then take the Cadillac. The Ford with the dead pharmaceutical salesman in the trunk had been in his possession long enough.

He pulled the Sig from his waistband and pressed his way through the rows of vegetables toward the woman.

She had pushed herself up to her hands and knees, backside facing him.

He brought the pistol up to his line of sight as she rolled over and pointed a hose of some sort at him.

His finger tightened on the trigger as the first blast of liquid hit his face. He heard the explosion from the muzzle of the Sig, felt the grip buck in his hand, but could see nothing.

The stench of the chemicals was overpowering, as if a thousand pounds of fertilizer and pesticides had been shoved up his nose.

The Professor dropped to the dirt and curled into a ball. He retched, and his half-digested breakfast dribbled out of the corner of his mouth. A sharp pain knifed across his thoracic cavity.

The product the woman had been spraying probably contained carbaryl, one of the few remaining organophosphate pesticides left on the market, or perhaps the recently banned diazinon. Both substances killed insects by preventing the neurotransmitter acetylcholine from doing its job in the nervous system, their respective chemical structures having been patterned on certain gases developed during World War II.

By the Nazis.

The Professor willed his heart to slow, his breathing to even out. He had sodium bicarbonate in his bag in the car, a neutralizing substance that would slow the reaction his body was experiencing. He wondered how many more exposures to such levels of toxins he could handle before his immune system cratered or his heart gave out.

He wiped liquid from his face, blinked several times, saw the woman a few feet away. Her eyes were open but unseeing. A thin stream of blood snaked across her forehead from the bullet hole a few centimeters above the bridge of her nose.

He pushed himself up on one arm and ran through the options. He would need to employ some freelance help now; too many in the Opposition were involved. He had a number for a Latino man who hired out the enforcers for his drug operation. For enough money, there would be no questions asked. He had to head west and mount an assault. He got up, cursing the frailties of his body.

He had to get out of there.

Because he hadn't found the contractor yet.

CHAPTER TWENTY-FOUR

Never bring a knife to a gunfight.

Rule One of gunfights.

Ryan Sherlock wobbled toward me with the automatic grasped tightly in his fingers while Petey locked the door to the Emerald Isle Saloon.

I kept the pint of Guinness in my hand, trying to see a way out of the situation that didn't involve violence.

Ryan stopped when he was three feet away and pointed the gun at my head. The lunchtime buzz had done a job on him. The muzzle wavered. His eyes were shiny like fresh dimes in the low light of the bar, feverish and watery with alcohol. Even in a smoky room, I could smell the whiskey on his breath.

"Why're you asking after my cousin?" His words slurred.

"Put the gun down." I took a sip of beer to show how nonchalant I was about the whole thing. "I think he might be in trouble."

"And how convenient, you just happening to know this," Petey said as he moved away from the door and stood by the jukebox. He was a string bean, all angles and bones and sinew, maybe five-five with a thin beard and freckled cheeks. He held his hands out, fists balled in a rough approximation of a boxer in the ring. Not exactly the way to do it in a bar fight, but I didn't figure Petey knew better.

"We just want to be left alone." Ryan shook the pistol at my nose, his face going maroon with anger. "But you country folk won't leave us be."

"I'm from Dallas." I smiled, trying to defuse the situation. "That's the big city, if you were wondering."

Petey said something, a few words in a language I didn't recognize. He took a couple of steps my way, hands still in a pugilist's stance.

Ryan blew air out of his mouth in a whoosh, cheeks tight against his teeth. The look in his eyes was disturbingly familiar, the stony glare a man gets just before he lets the monster in his soul loose upon the world.

I tossed beer in his face and leaned into him at the same instant, my left hand grabbing his right, my thumb slipping behind the trigger.

He reacted instinctively and pulled back.

I surprised him and went his direction, ramming my forehead into his nose. The impact made a crunching sound.

He fell backward.

I held on to the gun but let him fall. Unfortunately, his index finger was tangled in the trigger guard. He screamed as his digit snapped.

The jukebox switched music. Willie Nelson gave way to the Rolling Stones. "Gimme Shelter."

"What's a yonk?" I said. Petey put his hands up, palms out, face pasty white. The bartender and the other customer were both staring at me wide-eyed.

"Aye, look at him." Petey nodded toward where Ryan lay on the dirty floor. "Ya broke his nose, you did."

"He called me a yonk." I looked at the pistol. A Bersa, Brazilian made, .380-caliber. I flipped off the safety, racked the slide back, and saw a bullet in the chamber.

"You best be leaving," Petey said.

I shot the jukebox. Mick's singing stopped with a crash of glass and electronic components.

Petey went down on his knees, arms over his head.

"And why am I a country folk?"

Nobody answered.

I looked at Ryan huddled on the floor, moaning. The third customer was standing with his back pressed against the far wall, face ashen.

"A man came in last night," the bartender said. "He was asking after the Toogoode brothers."

"What did he look like?"

Ryan groaned.

"They're good boys, the Toogoodes." Petey licked his lips and looked at the injured man. "Hard workers."

"They were contractors, right?"

"What do you mean, were?"

"One of them is dead," I said quietly.

The bartender let out a loud sigh and placed his head in his hands.

"They're my cousins," Petey said. His eyes were flat, his tone hard.

"That mean they can't die?"

"How do we know you didn't kill him?"

"You don't." I looked at the bartender. "But it doesn't make much sense, me coming in here after taking one of them out."

Petey stared at me but didn't say anything.

"The guy last night is stalking a woman in Dallas," I said. "Terrorizing her and her daughter. Your cousins got in the way."

Petey looked at the bartender and nodded once.

"He didn't look like nothing," the bartender said.

"Thanks. That's a big help." I pointed the gun at a row of bottles behind the bar, maybe four or five grand worth of alcohol.

"I'm trying to tell you." The bartender raised one hand. "He was like a nobody, medium height, maybe a hundred and fifty pounds. Brown hair."

"What was he wearing?"

"I . . . I don't remember."

"That's not good enough." I closed one eye and aimed at a bottle of Bushmills. The bullet would take out an entire row of hooch.

"Put the gun down, mister." Petey jumped between the bottle and the muzzle of the .380. "Let's you and me go outside and have a little chat."

"Petey!" The bartender leaned against the bar, one arm outstretched. "Are you daft, man?"

"Probably so." Petey moved to the front door and unlocked it.

"We're gonna walk out together." I stepped away from the bar, gun still in my hand.

"You killed my jukebox." The bartender pointed to the machine, sparking and smoldering against the wall.

I shrugged and walked out, one hand on Petey's elbow, the other holding the .380 pressed against my thigh.

Once outside, Petey yanked free of my grip and turned around. He didn't say anything.

"You wanted to chat?" I stuck the gun in my back pocket.

"Leave us be."

Two guys on Harleys throttled by. I waited until they had passed. "All I'm interested in is the guy who came in asking questions."

Petey shook his head.

"I get him and I'll leave you alone. You guys can go back to whatever it is you got going on."

Petey closed his eyes.

"You're one of those Travelers, aren't you?" I pointed to the bar. "An Irish pub. Contractors. Supposed to be a bunch of you living together on the west side of town."

Travelers were a close-knit, clannish group of people of Celtic origin, almost tribal. They originally made their living as tinsmiths and knife sharpeners, the trade giving them one of their better-known names, tinkers. In the United States, they'd branched out into home repair, especially roofing and resurfacing asphalt. They traveled to ply the trade, hence the name. Another reason was to avoid the legal fall-out from some of the shoddy work performed. Most law enforcement officers I knew regarded them as being similar to Gypsies, that is, petty thieves and con artists, even though the Travelers were fair complected and bore no resemblance to the dark-skinned Roma.

"You don't understand us, so don't pretend." He crossed his arms.

"I don't care if you're running a flimflam on the queen of England. I just want to find the guy that came in last night."

"This is bad." Petey chewed on his lip and stared at nothing. "Brings attention to us."

I ejected the clip from the Bersa and removed the slide from the frame, then tossed all three pieces down a sewer grate.

"There's a place near here." He leaned against the wall by Bono's nose. "He might have gone there."

CHAPTER TWENTY-FIVE

Petey rode shotgun while I drove the VW, top still up and air-conditioning on high. He gave directions, zigzagging us across narrow residential streets in a more or less westerly direction. The houses in this section of Fort Worth were old and unkempt, yards filled with weeds, clapboard siding in need of fresh paint.

"What's your name?" Petey said as we passed an El Camino resting on cinder blocks.

"Oswald."

"And this woman you're helping. Why?"

"She hired me to." I slowed as a Hispanic man stooped with age pushed a wobbly ice cream cart across the street.

"So you're like an investigator?"

I nodded.

We were both silent for a few blocks. Then Petey said, "You ever think about doing something different?"

"Only on days that end in y."

"Ryan's a hothead, just so you know." Petey ignored my answer and stared out the window as the blighted core of Fort Worth, Texas, dribbled by. "He thinks all country folk are bad."

"What's a country folk?"

"You." Petey turned and looked at me as if I weren't getting a simple math problem. "An outsider."

"I don't get the country part."

He sighed. "You have a *country*. Not like us."

After fifteen minutes we came to a larger street, Las Vegas Trail. I stopped at the light.

"Turn right." Petey pointed to the north.

"Where are we going?"

"You'll know when we get there." He smoothed his hair back with one hand.

Ten minutes later I passed the city limit sign for White Settlement, a suburb on the western fringes of Fort Worth named long ago for the desired ethnicity of its population as opposed to the color of its buildings.

My navigator gave more directions, and pretty soon we were driving down a two-lane cul-de-sac, both sides of the street lined with pines and post oaks. At the end, a gate was partially open.

Petey hopped out of the VW, opened the chain-link gate wider, and motioned for me to enter.

I did so and found myself on the edge of a modest tract of land, maybe two acres, a small grove of live oaks in the middle, surrounded by a concrete street looping the entire property. To the right were six or eight houses, big and expensive-looking for this particular section of western Tarrant County, two-story brick structures with circular driveways surrounding fountains and outdoor statuary.

To the left was a series of driveways leading off the main street. At the end of each drive was a cluster of pipes sticking out of the ground. After a few moments, I figured out what they were: utility hookups for RVs.

But there were no Winnebagos or travel trailers parked there, just like there were no people anywhere.

Petey got back in the VW. "They've all gone."

"Where do you live?"

"Not here." His voice was tight.

The houses were gaudy, the paint on the trim a little too bright, the flowers a little too densely planted in colored plastic pots that flanked the front entrances ornate to the point of tacky.

"Oh sweet Mary." Petey grabbed my arm. "Stop the car."

He jumped out and ran away from the houses, toward a small cluster of trees and what looked like a vegetable garden.

I followed him. I passed a newish Ford Five Hundred parked underneath a live oak tree and stopped when I saw Petey kneeling beside the body of a woman.

She was dead. Her face was white and waxy except for the dark trail of blood across her forehead from the bullet hole.

Petey rocked back on his heels, face ashen. "That's Theresa, Sean's mother."

I nodded but didn't say anything.

"She's my cousin."

A spray bottle was on the ground a few feet from a small puddle of vomit covered with ants. Petey must have seen it at the same time. He jumped up.

"What the hell?" he said.

I looked at the dead woman. She'd dropped instantly from a bullet to the brain, too far away for the disgorged contents to be from her stomach. She could have tossed the bottle that far, or dropped it and vomited there only to die a few yards away, but her lips, a sickly purple now, were free of stomach debris.

"Did she . . ." Petey pointed at the puddle on the ground.

"I don't think so." I looked at the corpse and the Ford a few dozen feet away. "Our guy's a pro, but he loses his lunch over this? That doesn't make sense either."

Petey seemed to notice the car for the first time. He got up, walked over to it, and stopped, waving a hand in front of his face. "Cripes, something stinks."

I rattled the handle on the driver's side. The car was locked, windows up, but the odor was strong and reminded me of what the woman would smell like in a day or so of Texas heat. I picked up a rock the size of my fist, busted the driver's window, and popped the locks. I found the lever for the trunk by the front seat and pulled it.

The smell got infinitely worse. Petey covered his mouth with one hand. I tipped open the trunk with my foot and saw the bloated corpse there. Male. Age hard to determine. He'd been wearing a white dress shirt and tie, both of which were stained from the decomposition process. An open carton of what looked like pharmaceutical samples lay next to him. I slammed the trunk and jogged a few yards to get away from the smell.

"What the hell is going on?" Petey said.

"That makes three people this guy has taken out." I took deep breaths through my mouth.

"Why?"

"Because your cousins saw him when he didn't want to be seen. Now one of them is dead."

"What do I do now?"

"Where's your other cousin?"

Petey opened his mouth but didn't say anything.

"My guess is that he can ID the shooter," I said. "If I can get there first and find out what this guy looks like, your cousin might have a chance."

Petey shook his head.

"Okay, then call him."

The wind picked up, carrying with it the odor of rotting flesh.

"You don't grasp the situation, do you?" Petey said.

"I'm trying to save a life or two; what's so hard to understand about that?"

"You're a yonk and country folk," Petey sneered, "and we like to keep to our own. How many times do I gotta tell you?"

I rolled my shoulders and sighed. "You're gonna have to trust—"

"Screw you, yonk." A knife appeared in Petey's hand.

He lunged, the blade aimed at my stomach.

CHAPTER TWENTY-SIX

Knife fighting was a skill that Petey had yet to master fully.

I sidestepped the thrust, grabbing his wrist with one hand, bringing the elbow from my free arm up to his mouth. The blow wasn't hard, but it wasn't soft either. I felt his teeth gouge into my flesh.

Petey yelped, dropped the knife, and fell to the ground next to the Ford.

I grabbed the front of his shirt and yanked him to his feet. He stood in front of me, wobbly, both hands pressed against his mouth, eyes as round as half-dollars, skin pasty white except on his chin where the fresh blood meandered down.

"Aye, Petey, there'll be no kissing of the Blarney Stone for you tonight," I said.

"Uggh." His voice was muffled behind his hand.

"Here's the deal." I pulled harder on his shirt until our eyes were only inches apart. "There's a pro on the loose, and he's hurt or sick or something. That's a very bad thing, kind of like a wounded lion you'd see on the Discovery Channel."

"W-w-what do you want?"

"This should be review, but let's go over it again." I let go of the shirt and grabbed his neck. "Collin Toogoode."

"No. Not a chance." Petey shook his head. Blood from his lip splattered on my hand. "We don't like outsiders messing in our affairs. It's been this way for centuries."

"Petey, are you stupid?" I forced him to look at the dead woman. "An outsider is already here. I'm trying to stop him."

"Jaysus, would you let me think." He began to shake as if he were cold.

I let go of him with a shove.

He stumbled a few feet and then ran, heading for the nearest house.

"Aw, nuts." I kicked at the dirt before taking off after him.

He had about a thirty-foot head start. I was taller and faster and caught him when he got to the front door of a beige brick home with statues of Pluto and Dumbo in the front yard.

I dove and tackled him and together we fell into the door, knocking it open. I landed on a pink marble floor with Petey on top of me. The tile was cold and hard where it connected with my temple.

Petey jacked his elbow into my stomach. I curled into a ball for a moment, waiting for oxygen to return. When I had my breath, the entryway was empty.

"Petey?" I walked into the living room, wheezing. "Where the hell are you?"

No response.

The main living area of the house was decorated in neo-disco revival. White shag carpet. Maroon velour sectional sofas along two walls, bracketing an oval-shaped piece of smoked glass resting on a brass wagon wheel. The air smelled like cinnamon and vanilla and stale cigar smoke.

The highlight of the room was a picture of the pope.

On black velvet.

"*Petey.*" I cupped my hands and shouted toward the stairway. "I'm not leaving."

A floorboard creaked upstairs.

I figured Petey was contained for the moment, so I did a quick search of the ground floor. A dining room with more white shag and smoked glass.

One bedroom with a waterbed and an orange, zebra-patterned comforter.

A kitchen with neon green cabinets.

One corner of the kitchen had been set up as a tiny office. Papers were scattered everywhere, some trampled on the floor. Since the rest of the place was clean and tidy, I started there.

I found current bills for electric service and water for A. Carroll, a payment due notice for a landline in the name of Carroll Remodeling, and not much else personalized other than catalogs for various mail order houses that specialized in gaudy clothes and cheap makeup.

No cell phone records. No bills from the cable company to go with the big-screen TV in the living room.

I found several spiral-bound notebooks filled with a tightly written script in a weird English hybrid language. Some words, mostly verbs, were recognizable.

More creaking floorboards from upstairs. I would have to deal with Petey pretty soon.

I returned my attention to the notebooks. On the last page of the last book I read the words "flowers" and "weather f." along with gibberish. I tossed them aside and stood up.

A phone with a long cord was mounted on the far wall, next to a small dry-erase board. I walked over and picked up the handset. No dial tone. A few lines of writing were on the board.

"Marty." I said the name out loud. "In Weather . . . fd." A phone number with an area code I couldn't identify followed.

Weather. Again.

Marty was in some weather. Which made no sense . . . unless it did.

"Marty in Weather," I said. "Weather. Ford. Texas."

Weatherford was a town about an hour west of Fort Worth. I entered the phone number into my cell but didn't call. I headed to the stairs.

"Hey, Petey. I'm leaving now."

Nothing. Not even a creak.

"I found the address."

The compressor on the refrigerator kicked on but still no sound from upstairs.

"I'm headed to Weatherford."

Footsteps shuffled then stopped.

I clomped to the front door and slammed it shut but stayed inside.

Hurried steps down the stairs.

I pressed against the wall that was out of view from the rest of the house, willing myself to become at one with the lemon-yellow flocked wall covering.

Petey dashed into the foyer, a revolver in his fist. He noticed me at the same instant that I grabbed the hand holding the weapon and twisted it up behind his back.

"You weren't going to shoot me, were you?" I whispered in his ear.

He didn't respond. His breathing was ragged. He smelled of sweat and beer.

"I don't want to hurt you." I eased the pressure on his arm a little.

"Everybody wants to hurt us." His voice was tight.

"More of your people are going to die unless this guy is stopped."

"You can't go to Weatherford." His voice was choked with emotion.

"Yes, Petey. I most certainly can go to Weatherford." I wrenched the gun from his hand and shoved him against the wall.

"They'll kill you."

"No, they won't." I shook my head. "Your people run scams; they don't do the violence thing very well. Neither do you. Your heart's not in it."

"If I take you, then they'll kill me."

"I can live with that."

CHAPTER TWENTY-SEVEN

The Texas of myth and legend lay spread before us, a vast sheet of undulating earth reaching westward to a horizon so all-encompassing it threatened to overwhelm the senses and the ability to describe.

The surface of the terrain was the color of aged straw except for the occasional patch of green and the black-gray of the fence lines running like scars across the land. Farmhouses, stock tanks, and the occasional oil well seesawing crude from the depths dotted the sunbaked ground.

We were on Interstate 20, a dozen miles east of Weatherford, riding together in silence in the Volkswagen, a tiny ship lost amid a sea of eighteen-wheelers, pickups, and Suburbans.

About the time we'd passed the western limits of Tarrant County, I had given up trying to make Petey talk. He sat in the passenger seat, nursing his swollen mouth and sullen attitude.

Born under a bad sign, those Irish Travelers were.

I remembered what I could of the mysterious group. Most of my information was apocryphal, beer-fueled anecdotes from bunko cops. The Travelers ran half-assed shakedown scams. Slip-and-fall claims on insurance. Money accepted for contracting work never done. Several years ago a Traveler woman had tried to extort money from Disney World with a fabricated rape story.

They spoke their own language, too, as I recalled, a hybrid tongue derived from the ancient Celtic dialect.

Above anything else, they possessed an overwhelming desire to be left alone, a quality I could identify with all too well.

As a truck loaded with cattle rocketed past us, I said, "You never told me what a yonk is."

"It's our term for a crook." Petey blew a jet of air out of the corner of his mouth.

"Wasn't there a Toogoode that got caught on tape beating her child?" I said. "Somewhere in the Midwest, a couple of years ago."

Petey paused for a long time before replying. "Yeah."

"She any relation to Collin?"

"Something wrong with that girl." Petey shook his head. "Hitting a child like that."

"You got any kids?" I maneuvered around a slow-moving truck and flatbed trailer loaded with hay.

He didn't reply.

"You married?"

"She told who her people were. She ain't welcome back."

"What's gonna happen when you show up with me?"

He pulled a cell phone from his pocket. As he flipped it open, I put one hand on his arm.

"If you call and set something up where I'm the fall guy, the first person to get it is you." I glanced down for a half second to where the revolver he'd been carrying was resting on the floorboard underneath my seat.

"You don't have much trust in your heart, do you?" he said.

"The Travelers aren't the only ones that like a low profile."

He pulled his arm free from my grasp and dialed a number. He held the phone to his ear for a long time before hitting the end button. "We may be too late."

The Travelers had come to America in the middle of the nineteenth century, among the first wave of Irish immigrants escaping the potato famine, Petey told me.

After the Civil War, they'd wandered about the land, settling in different areas, the largest group in a compound north of the Savannah River called Murphy Village, after a priest of the same name who convinced a large group of Travelers to buy property there.

The Irish Travelers of Texas were known as the Greenhorn Carrolls and had made White Settlement their primary headquarters until an automobile accident one New Year's Eve involving several Traveler children forced part of the clan to move west to avoid scrutiny by the authorities.

I asked why he'd told me all this, but he wouldn't say, shaking his head slowly and staring out the window at the strip malls, barbecue joints, and used car lots that formed the outskirts of Weatherford, Texas.

Petey again gave directions, and pretty soon we were at our destination.

The Greenhorn Carrolls lived in a true compound; the chain-link fence had barbed wire on top running around several acres of land.

I stopped by the gate and watched smoke billow toward the sky.

"Oh no." Petey leaned across the dashboard and peered through the window. "He's already here."

Two gunshots rattled in the distance.

He looked at me.

"How many people live in there?" I pulled off the road to one side of the gate.

"Not many now. Maybe ten or so. Maybe less. Mostly women." Petey jumped out of the car. "Everybody's on the road this time of year, earning."

I grabbed the weapon off the floorboard. It was a Smith & Wesson revolver, a four-inch-barrel .38-caliber. Fully loaded with six bullets, 158-grain roundnose lead. I'd have given Petey's Rolex for a little more firepower, but that wasn't going to happen.

"Let's go." I slipped through the gate. The Weatherford compound was heavily wooded, live oaks and cottonwoods thick with vines. A dirt road led to the right.

I jogged down the path, gun in my hand, Petey running behind me.

The road veered to the left. About twenty feet ahead, a man in a gray track suit stepped out of the woods. He was about seven feet tall, bald like a cue ball, carrying a shotgun in one hand. The firearm looked like a child's toy in his grasp.

He raised the weapon and pointed it at me.

I stopped but kept the gun in my hand. Petey almost rammed into my back.

"Oswald, right?" the man said.

"Yeah." I frowned, trying to remember where and in what context I knew this elephantine human being. There had been so many lowlifes over so many years. Hard to recollect exactly. Plus, I had made a conscious decision to try to forget.

"What are you doing here?" He lowered the shotgun slightly, the muzzle pointing at my knees now.

"Working." I smiled and shrugged as the man's name came to me.

Bobby Ray. A low-rent enforcer for a thug in Fort Worth who ran the gambling and hookers on the south side of town. Bobby Ray had once tossed a prostitute through a plate glass window on Christmas Day. That was the good story I remembered about him.

"Heard you got out of the life." He put the shotgun back to his shoulder. "Now you're here."

"A man's gotta make a living, you know?" I cocked my head to one side. "Guy called, said he needed help with a bunch of Gypsies."

"We're right in the middle of it." He laughed and lowered the gun again. "Greasy little fuckers scream a lot when you torch their trailers."

Petey let out a groan and stepped out from behind me.

The gigantic man frowned. "Who's that?"

"Nobody."

"You're not working for my team, are you?" He raised the shotgun, finger tightening around the trigger.

"The hell I'm not. You think I'd come all the way out here and—" I shot Bobby Ray in the chest.

He looked at the wound in his sternum and then at me. He tightened his grip on the shotgun and squinted down the barrel.

"Holy shit." Petey crossed himself.

I fired again. The bullet hit a few centimeters from the first.

Bobby Ray dropped the gun and sat down on the dirt path, cross-legged. He stared at me and then at Petey and clutched his chest. A few drops of blood flecked his lips.

I grabbed the shotgun from the ground and a nickel-plated revolver from the front of his waistband. We now had three firearms between us.

"Here." I tossed Petey the handgun.

He caught the weapon by the barrel, held on to it for a nanosecond, and then dropped it as if it were on fire.

"I don't like guns," he said.

"Me neither." I picked up the gun and pointed toward the direction of the smoke. "Let's go."

The Professor smiled inside the face mask strapped across his nose and chin, the flow of oxygen gentle as it wafted across the tender membranes of his nasal cavity. Between the pure O_2 and the antioxidants he'd taken, he had mitigated some but not all of the damage done by the Traveler woman and her pesticide spray.

He stood behind a large elm tree in the woods a few dozen yards or so from where the strange man from the house in Plano had just dispatched the lummox named Bobby Ray.

Lee Henry Oswald.

A warrior, much like himself, a veteran of the elder Bush's Middle Eastern campaign, according to an old contact at the U.S. Army Human Resources Center in St. Louis.

And, if the child was to be believed, an employee of his target, Anita Nazari.

A Ranger. A worthy opponent if only his health had been better. Now he would have to use stealth and artifice.

Later, if time and circumstances permitted, he would enjoy a visit with the man, a chance to learn how he had made it to the Gypsy encampment. A comparing of notes after the game, so to speak. He hoped he wouldn't have to kill him.

A voice sounded in his earpiece, the one hired freelancer with an IQ above that of farm animal. The quarry, the second contractor, had been spotted.

The Professor stepped away from the tree and slipped deeper into the woods.

CHAPTER TWENTY-EIGHT

Petey led the way this time, holding the shotgun awkwardly against his chest. I followed a few steps behind, carrying the Smith against my thigh.

"I've never seen anybody get killed before," Petey said.

"Hope you don't ever again." I could see flames through the trees now. "But I wouldn't count on it."

We reached the edge of the wooded area. Four large travel trailers were visible, double wheeled, triple axled. Expensive looking.

Three were on fire. The fourth was closest, maybe seventy-five or eighty yards away. The air smelled like somebody had dropped a Styrofoam cup full of urine into a fire pit of burning rubber. Oily and nasty, choke-inducing from the plastics and other synthetic materials that were aflame.

Three men stood by the last trailer, talking to each other. Each held a long gun of some kind, either a rifle or a shotgun.

I pulled Petey behind a thick old pecan tree, bracketed on either side by oak saplings. "You recognize any of those guys?"

He shook his head.

"You wouldn't by any chance have any military experience?"

"Don't even have a Social Security number." He turned and looked at me. "You think I'd join your nation's army?"

One of the men by the RV bent over with laughter. Another slapped him on the back and pointed to the surviving RV. The third fired his weapon in the air. It was a rifle. The sharp crack of the report hit my ears a split second after a finger of smoke jetted out of the barrel.

"There's only women and children here." Petey hopped from one foot to the other.

I studied the terrain and vegetation. The woods curved to our left, toward the burning trailers. If you followed the trees, you might get as close as thirty or forty yards to the group of men, at the extreme range of the shotgun. They'd get peppered by pellets. And mightily pissed off.

A .38-caliber bullet could be deadly that far away, but wildly inaccurate out of a four-inch barrel. I grabbed the second revolver, the one I'd taken off of Bobby Ray, from Petey's grasp.

"Hey." He resisted for a moment before letting go.

The gun was an old Colt Trooper Mark III, again in the wimpy .38 caliber, though this time loaded with six hollowpoints.

I turned my attention to the shotgun, a Remington 11-87 with a magazine extension tube bolted onto the forearm, making the weapon look almost like a double barrel. I jacked the bolt back and ejected a shell, repeating the movement until the gun was empty.

Four red shells lay on the carpet of leaves at my feet. I picked them up. Double-ought buckshot. A dozen or so ball-bearing-sized hunks of lead in each.

I reloaded and handed it back to Petey. The shotgun was a much superior weapon for close-in combat, but four shells didn't leave much margin for error. I would take the two .38s with ten bullets between them and hope my meager pistol-shooting skills would be up to the challenge if it came to that.

More laughing from the men by the RV. Waving guns at the trailer.

I recognized the action for what it was, an adrenaline bleed-off, the let-down after a firefight.

One of the men fired again, and even from the distance I heard a woman scream.

Petey said something in his language and lunged toward the clearing. I grabbed his shirt and pulled him to the ground before he got away from the cover.

"Suicide is not the answer." I dragged him back behind the tree. "This sounds stupid, but let's synchronize our watches."

He frowned.

"What time do you have?" I grabbed his wrist, looked at the gaudy gold Rolex. Four sixteen. I adjusted my Timex to the same minute.

"You're gonna take the shotgun and walk along the tree line that way." I nodded to the left. "When you get to the point closest to the bad guys, stop."

Petey gave me a blank stare.

"Got that?"

He blinked once and nodded.

"Good. That should take you about three minutes, give or take." I tapped my watch. "So let's say that at exactly four twenty, you fire at those guys. Shoot twice and then run as fast as possible in the opposite direction."

"Four twenty." He nodded. "Shoot twice."

"That's correct," I said. "That will leave two more bullets for when they follow. You know the compound pretty well, right? You can find a place to hide?"

"Yeah, I can lose them, don't worry." He shrugged his shoulders and rolled his head like a runner loosening up for a track meet. "But what about you?"

"Don't worry." I smiled tightly. "I've got a plan."

CHAPTER TWENTY-NINE

I had no plan.

Petey took off, moving quietly through the underbrush.

I stood behind the tree for a full minute, trying to figure out what to do. The smartest course of action would be to get back to the VW and leave. I owed nothing to these bizarre Traveler people, nor to Anita Nazari.

But a strange thing had happened during the confrontation with Bobby Ray and the surreptitious hike through the wooded compound.

I got the juice back. I was loose and wired and cold inside, all at the same time.

Everything was more distinct now, the unevenness of the ground against my feet, the tiny details of the lichen on the oak trees, the crackle and roar of the burning trailers. I could feel the individual lines checkering the grip of the Smith in my palm.

I wanted to kick some ass and write home to Mom about it. Nolan was right; the juice was good. I hated her for pointing it out.

The group of men laughed and whooped, a bottle passing among them now. Three soldiers without a captain.

I stepped out of the clearing, looked at my watch. Two and a half minutes to go.

I stuck the revolvers in the waistband of my jeans, one behind each hip. I pulled out my cell phone and placed it against my head, mouthing into it, gesticulating with my free hand while staring at the three men as I walked.

They were drinking and laughing and watching the trailer, so I made it to within twenty yards before one turned around and saw me.

He wore a fedora with the brim pulled down, warm-up pants, sneakers, and a shiny bicycle chain dangling around his neck on top of a white T-shirt.

I nodded hello and continued to talk and move closer.

He said something to the other two.

I stopped when I was about ten feet away, still jabbering into the cell phone. I swore and mentioned the name of a man in Dallas who controlled most of the narcotics and all of the prostitution in the eastern half of the county, and how he could go perform an anatomical impossibility on himself.

All three were looking at me now. The one on the end, a fat guy in a Troy Aikman Cowboys jersey, had raised his gun. He lowered it when he heard the name mentioned.

"Heya, homes." Fedora squinted at me from under the brim of his hat. "What the hell are you doing?"

I smiled and gave him that on-the-phone-gimme-a-second look, holding one finger in the air.

"I'm talking to you." Fedora's eyes got big, his voice louder and impatient.

"Hold on a minute, willya?" I spoke into the empty phone before pressing it against my chest. To Fedora and company, I said, "Do you jerkoffs have any idea of the shit you're in on account of this little action today?"

Fedora frowned. Troy Aikman cocked his head to one side.

I looked at my watch. Forty-five seconds to go. I put the phone back to my ear. "Yeah, you were right. These guys are beyond stupid. Must be something in the water in Fort Worth. I gotta go." I ended the fake call and turned to the men. "Who's running your crew?"

"Before we get to that," Fedora said, "suppose you tell us who you are."

"You went freelance." I shook my head. "Without getting clearance."

"Clearance?" Troy Aikman scratched an ear. "The fuck you talking about, bro?"

"The guy that hired you. There's a slight problem."

Troy Aikman looked at Fedora, who looked at the third guy and then at the trailer. The afternoon wind shifted and a cloud of black smoke blew between the three goons and me.

"There're people above you on the food chain," I said, "and they are mighty pissed."

"The boss said it was cool." Fedora licked his lips. "Guy paid cash."

The third goon, an older man in a pair of jeans and an untucked denim shirt, eased away from the other two, toward the tree line, in a flanking move.

"Where's the guy that hired you?" I looked at my watch. Fifteen seconds to go.

"Out there somewhere." Troy Aikman shrugged.

"What's in the trailer?" I nodded toward the Winnebago that wasn't burning.

"Split tail, bro." Fedora grinned. "Gonna have us a party. Spoils of war and shit."

Troy Aikman laughed and grabbed his crotch.

I heard the buckshot whiz by a millisecond before the report of the shotgun echoed across the compound. The older guy yelped, grabbed his face, and fell to the ground.

Fedora and Troy dropped, too, as did I, right as the second blast ripped through the air.

"Shit," Troy said.

"Fuck," Fedora said back.

"Told you some people were mighty pissed off." I elbowed my way closer to Fedora.

Troy hopped up on one knee and fired at the tree line with the fully automatic M-16 he'd been carrying.

"What did the guy look like?" I tapped Fedora on the leg.

"What?" He turned from the trees and looked at me.

"The guy that hired you."

"Average-looking dude. Not young, not old. Nothing particular about him except the funny glasses."

"Glasses?"

"Had like a mirror or some shit on them."

"Ohh, my eye," the third man wailed.

Something in the trailer farthest away exploded, showering the area with burning Winnebago parts and more black smoke.

"Cover me." Troy Aikman fired another burst into the trees. He got up and ran a zigzag pattern toward a small shed by one of the burning trailers.

"Cover you, my ass." Fedora popped his head up, looked around. "The hell he think this is, a 50 Cent video?"

Troy disappeared into the woods.

"I can't see anything." The third man stood up, one hand over his eye, blood streaming down his face. After a few seconds, he fell over and huddled in a ball.

"Sucks to be you, don't it?" Fedora said to his compatriot before turning to me. "That was a shotgun that fired at us."

I didn't reply.

"Lucky to hit my boy in the face with a scattergun from that far away." Fedora pushed himself to his feet, keeping his rifle pointed to the ground.

I got up, too, but didn't say anything. I pulled the Colt from my waistband and held it by my side.

"Means the dog out there shooting at us ain't a pro." He cocked his head toward the woods. We were about five feet apart.

"Good point." I nodded. Fedora was not nearly as stupid as I wanted him to be. "But I *am* a pro. And you do not want to turn on the lights and find out what I'm selling."

"Shit, brother." The man smiled. "Think you could take me?"

I looked suddenly toward the Winnebago, as if I had heard something, and moved in with my left shoulder. Grabbed his hand holding the rifle with my left. Smashed the side of his fedora with my right, the barrel of the Colt connecting with a soft thud against the felt of his hat.

He went down on his side, groaning. I held on to the rifle. I ejected the magazine, saw it was empty, and jacked open the chamber. Empty, too.

"Hey, *bro*." I tossed the weapon as far as possible toward one of the burning trailers. "Looks like you're out of bullets."

Fedora pushed himself up on his hands and knees.

I walked to where the third man lay and found his weapon. A Benelli assault shotgun. I slung it over my shoulder and returned to Fedora, who was trying to stand up. I put a foot on his rib cage and shoved him over.

He looked at me without speaking.

"Tell me about the guy." I pointed the Smith at him. "What was he wearing? How did he contact you?"

"He had on, like, khakis, you know." Fedora rolled himself over and sat on the ground, holding one hand pressed against his head. "And a T-shirt. Dorky-looking dude, you ask me."

"Keep going." I looked at the tree line but saw no sign of Troy or Petey or anybody else.

"Boss called. Said a guy was coming here, recommended by some people connected to Ari in Dallas."

I grinned for a moment. Everybody in the life knew Ari, a four-and-a-half-foot-tall Armenian psychopath who ran a casino and bordello in the back room of a bar in East Dallas. The good thing about Ari was he would give up his grandmother to the Hell's Angels for the right motivation.

Fedora got up as another explosion ripped through the air, billowing out a cloud of black smoke that reminded me of nothing so much as the oil field fires in the Kuwaiti desert almost twenty years ago.

"You leave now, you get to live," I said.

He stared at me for a long few moments before walking to where his partner lay and helping him stand. Together they limped toward the road leading out.

After a few feet, Fedora stopped and turned around. "Guy was some kind of crazy, too."

"Yeah?"

He nodded. "Went all apeshit when he saw a can of Raid in the back of my pickup."

"What's that about?"

"Hell if I know." He shrugged. "Dude was all 'environmental toxic' this, and 'poison that' kinda shit. Weird-ass sunuvabitch, let me tell you." He took a step toward the road but stopped again. "You and me," he said. "We ain't through."

"Sorry, bro." I shook my head. "We most certainly are through."

CHAPTER THIRTY

I watched Fedora and the third man limp down the road leading out of the compound. I figured I didn't have much time before they found another gun or their boss got involved. For a moment I wondered how Petey was faring in the woods with Troy Aikman chasing him. Petey was a big boy; he could take care of himself.

When they were out of sight, I started to turn to the surviving Winnebago but a movement at the edge of the woods caught my eye. A quick flash of neon red against the brown of the tree trunk. I took one glance at the trailer, grabbed the Benelli, and headed toward the woods at a run.

The acrid smoke caught in my throat about midway to the tree line. By the time I got to the place where I thought I had seen movement, I was hacking and wheezing like a three-pack-a-day smoker struggling up Kilimanjaro.

I leaned against a tree and coughed up a section of lung. When my breathing returned more or less to normal, I strained to hear movement and peered into the woods.

Nothing to hear but the burning Winnebagos crackling and popping, and the ringing in my ears from the gunfire earlier. Nothing to see but trees and undergrowth, a canvas of earth tones, the only movement coming from the swaying of the vegetation in the wind.

I put my hand on the tree to push off but yanked it back, spots of blood dappling my palm from the thorny vine growing on the trunk.

A shot rang out, the direction of the sound hard to pinpoint because of the thick undergrowth.

I left the shotgun at the edge of the wooded area, the brush so thick as to render it useless, and headed toward where I thought the shot came from. I pushed brush away with one hand, pulled out Bobby Ray's .38 with the other.

After twenty yards or so I stepped into a small clearing about half the size of a basketball court. At regular intervals a series of stone markers dotted a portion of the area. I knelt by the nearest one and saw that it was marked in an alphabet I didn't recognize.

The numbers were readable, though, and left no doubt as to what I had stumbled upon.

A Traveler cemetery.

I walked through the tombstones, doing a rough count. Maybe thirty or forty graves. As I reached the end of the graveyard, a coughing spasm erupted from deep within my chest. I dropped Bobby Ray's pistol and bent over, hands on my knees, struggling to get enough oxygen in my lungs.

When I looked up, the muzzle of a Beretta pistol was pointed at my face, about ten feet away. The man holding the weapon was Hispanic, in his midthirties, wearing jeans, combat boots, and a brown T-shirt.

"Don't move."

I held up my hands. The second revolver was in my back pocket, not visible to the man with the Beretta.

"Step away from the gun." The man nodded to Bobby Ray's pistol lying on the ground.

"I've got backup nearby." My words didn't even sound convincing to me.

He ignored me and pulled a walkie-talkie from his belt and spoke a few words into it, too indistinct for me to hear. A staticy voice replied, and thirty seconds later two figures appeared from the woods on the far side of the clearing.

The first man was handcuffed, wearing a red windbreaker with the words TOOGOODE CONSTRUCTION on the breast. He'd been hit several times in the face, cheeks bruised and bleeding, one eye blackened. A strip of masking tape had been stuck across his mouth.

Behind him came a figure carrying an H&K MP5 machine gun, wearing what appeared to be a camouflaged hazmat suit complete with oxygen tank and full-face mask like the ones used by Everest climbers. He shoved the bound man to the ground and stepped to where I had dropped the revolver.

Nobody said anything. The only sound in the clearing was the wheeze of the respirator attached to his oxygen mask.

He kept the machine gun pointed my way but bent over and retrieved the .38 with one gloved hand.

"Who are you?" I said.

In one smooth motion he stood upright, pointed the muzzle of the .38 at the Hispanic man's temple, and squeezed the trigger.

"What the—" I flinched at the noise echoing through the trees and the spray of blood misting languidly on the slight breeze in the clearing.

The man on the ground gyrated, trying to stand, groaning through the masking tape, his eyes wide.

"Hands on top of your head." Hazmat's voice sounded like Darth Vader's through the oxygen mask.

I did as requested.

"With the thumb and forefinger on your left hand, remove the pistol in your back pocket."

I didn't move.

"Or I'll shoot you in the crotch."

I pulled the revolver from my pocket in the method he'd suggested.

"Toss it behind you."

After I had complied, he walked to where the bound man lay and shot him twice in the back of the head with the .38. He turned to where I stood, still with my hands in the air.

"A sad but necessary ending for Mr. Collin Toogoode," he said.

"What about me?"

"You don't know who I am, nor do you have any way to ID me." He dropped the .38 into a plastic bag. "But I'll keep this for insurance." He held the bag up high. "Looks like it even has some of your blood on the grip."

I felt the two small wounds on my palm from the thorns earlier.

"That will give the DNA boys something fun to play with." He cocked his head toward the sound of a shotgun blast not too far away. "My, er, associates might have other plans for you, though."

"Why are you after Anita Nazari?"

"Don't be stupid and follow me." He kept the MP5 pointed my way and walked backward to the edge of the clearing before turning and vanishing into the bramble.

Several shots sounded in the wood; a bullet splintered into a tree on the far side from where I stood. I turned the opposite way the hazmat man had gone and ran, picking up the shotgun at the edge of the clearing.

The surviving Winnebago was where I'd last seen it, and I headed that way. The vehicle was huge, as big as a Greyhound bus. A brown and gold awning matching the RV's paint job was stretched over a makeshift patio consisting of a couple of plastic lawn chairs, a Weber charcoal grill, and a faded Igloo cooler.

What looked like the main entrance to the vehicle was underneath the awning, too, next to a window starburst by a bullet.

A curtain twitched in the window.

I wondered how much they had seen of what had just occurred. I wondered whether they would trust me or not.

I knocked on the door.

No answer.

"I'm not going to hurt you." I rapped again. "They're not far behind me. We don't have much time."

Nothing.

"I'm a friend of Petey's." That was stretching it, but I figured under the circumstances it wouldn't hurt.

The lock rattled. The door opened a crack, and half of a woman's face appeared in the gap. She was in her late thirties with reddish hair. Freckles on a long thin nose. Pale green eyes.

"You need to get out of here." I pointed to the woods. "They're gonna come back."

"Who are you?" the woman said.

"My name is Oswald. I'm a friend."

She raised one eyebrow a millimeter, a gesture that spoke volumes about her view of trust and friends.

An automatic weapon chattered in the distance, sounding like Troy's M-16. I hoped Petey was okay.

"How do I know you're not one of them?" The woman nodded toward the trees.

"You don't," I said. "You're gonna have to trust me."

"We're not big on trust around here." She spat the words out.

"Then you can end up like Toogoode." I turned and walked away.

"Wait."

The door slammed shut. I turned around.

"What do you know about my husband?" The woman stood underneath the awning. She wore a pair of khaki shorts, a white blouse, and too much makeup. I revised the age downward a little, maybe thirty-five.

"He worked with his brother, didn't he?" I spoke softly, unsure of how to handle meeting the wife.

She nodded.

"Who showed up here yesterday?" I said. "Your husband or his brother?"

"My brother-in-law." Her voice was a whisper.

The front door of the Winnebago opened, and a child about eight or nine years old stepped outside. She was dressed like a prepubescent call girl. Rhinestone-encrusted blouse. Tight red skirt. Hair teased into a big pouffy ball on top, long and flowing on the sides.

And makeup.

Lots and lots of makeup, more than you'd see on a sixty-year-old cocktail waitress in Vegas. Pink rouge and red lip gloss and purple eyeshadow, all thickly slathered on the child's face.

"Mama, is Daddy back?" She clutched a doll under her arm.

The woman turned her head and spoke to the child. "Mary, go back inside."

"Who's that?" The girl stared at me with wide eyes.

The woman spoke in the Traveler language. The anger in her tone was clear, and the girl darted back to the interior of the RV.

"Your husband and his brother had a job in Plano this past weekend, didn't they?" I said.

She nodded, tears welling in her hazel eyes.

"But only your brother-in-law came back, and then all hell breaks loose today."

"Collin wouldn't say what happened." She closed her eyes tightly.

"Patrick have a U2 concert T-shirt?"

She nodded.

"I'm sorry."

"No. Can't be." Her voice was a whisper.

I shook my head slowly, feeling the grief come off her in a wave.

"He was a decent man." Tears streamed down her face. "A good provider."

"I'm sure he was," I said. "He was in the wrong place at the wrong time."

More gunfire, closer this time. A few seconds later another explosion ripped from one of the trailers. More black smoke, burning debris, a surreal battlefield on the plains of northwest Texas.

"Will this thing drive?" I pointed to the Winnebago.

"We can't leave without Collin."

"He can't be helped right now," I said.

"What do you mean?"

"He's not coming back either." I didn't know what else to say.

"Oh, no. Not him, too." Her eyes filled with fresh tears. "He slipped out when the first ones showed up, said it was him they wanted and that we'd be okay if he was gone."

"He was wrong. None of us will be okay if we stay around here."

She sat down in the lawn chair and sobbed.

"What's your name?"

"Bria." She rubbed her nose with the back of her hand. "Bria Toogoode."

"You know Petey?"

"Yeah. Black Petey Gorman. He's my cousin."

"Petey brought me to this place to help Collin. I failed, but the least I can do is get you out of here."

"I can't." She shook her head. "You're an outsider; it doesn't work that way."

"Whatever is going on is liable to get worse before it gets better." I pointed to the burning trailers and black smoke.

She turned and opened the door. "C'mon in."

The inside was decorated like a typical motor home, which, come to think of it, was not that far from how the gaudy house in White

Settlement had been furnished: lots of shag carpets, loud colors, laminated wood, and smoked glass.

Three other people were sitting in the main living area on a white leather sectional sofa.

The young girl, Mary, who'd just been outside.

A grandmother type, somewhere in that indeterminate age between ninety and a hundred and fifty, her hair as white as paint on a funeral home, eyes cloudy.

And a woman about Bria's age. She had bright green eyes and dirty blond hair and wore jeans so tight they appeared to be painted on and a sleeveless black blouse. By anybody's definition, she was gorgeous, carrying herself with a certain haughty sexuality I'd seen during a thousand lost nights in bars the world over.

Without thinking about it, I sucked in my stomach a little and ran a couple of fingers through my hair.

She stood up. Looked at me and then at Bria. "What's going on?"

Bria waved her away and sat down on a chair by the door, fresh tears staining her cheeks.

The second Traveler woman looked back at me, growled, and lunged, nails splayed, knees and elbows looking for soft spots.

We went down on the shag carpet, me pressing my legs together and ducking my head, her screaming.

"Let me explain." I tried to grasp at least one limb to stem the attack.

Slap. Scratch. Kick.

"I'm trying to help." I got hold of an elbow, squeezed right above the joint. The woman moaned and tried to wriggle free. I was behind her now, one hand maintaining pressure on the sensitive nerves of her arm, the other going for a bear hug.

"Let me go." She went for my shins with her heels.

I squeezed harder on her arm.

She stopped fighting, and we lay on the floor spooning in a lovers' embrace. I could smell the shampoo she'd used that morning, the faint soapy odor mixing with perfume and sweat.

"I'm gonna let you go," I said, "and you're not gonna fight anymore, okay?"

She didn't say anything, breathing shallow and rapid.

I pressed harder still on the elbow.

"All right all right." She nodded.

I let go and pushed her away.

She jumped up and ran over to the sofa.

I stood, wobbly, feeling for additional contusions.

The old woman and the girl hadn't moved.

"Who knows how to drive this thing?" I said.

"I do," Bria said.

The room was quiet for a few moments.

Finally the woman on the sofa said, "You're a traitor, Bria. Bringing him in here like this."

"He's not one of those who was shooting at us." Bria moved to the window and peered out before jumping back suddenly. "And it looks like they're back."

CHAPTER THIRTY-ONE

The window disappeared in a shower of safety glass as a boom blasted through the interior of the RV, followed by wind and smoke from the fires. Somebody was using a shotgun at close range, and I bet it wasn't Petey.

Bria fell to the floor, screaming.

Her daughter hugged the grandmother and whimpered.

The woman who had attacked me slid off the sofa onto the floor and belly-crawled toward the front of the RV. When she was even with where I lay, she pointed to the shotgun on my shoulder. "You know how to use that thing?"

I nodded and crawled to the window. Popped the safety off. Swung the barrel out.

Two guys I'd never seen before were about twenty yards away, each holding a weapon. The Backup was here.

I fired twice, pulling the trigger on the Benelli so quickly that the reports sounded like one long blast. I thought one of the men dropped, but it was hard to tell because the Winnebago lurched forward as the echo from the second shot died, and the awning tore away, blocking my view.

The RV hit a hole or something. My head whammed into the window frame, embedding three or four chunks of glass in my temple as well as disorienting me for a few seconds.

More bumps. Women yelling. Swearing.

I got up and grabbed the back of a captain's chair bolted to the floor.

Bria was holding her daughter now, both crying.

I staggered to the front and fell into the passenger's seat.

The woman swore and yanked the wheel to the left. It was hard to see what she was trying to miss, as the view was all but completely obscured by smoke.

"Damn you, yonks." She jerked the wheel to the right.

"Where are you going?" I braced myself as we hit another chuckhole.

She didn't say anything, her knuckles white on the steering wheel, lips tight across her teeth, eyes unblinking.

The smoke cleared, and I realized what she was doing. Immediately in front of us were the two men, one obviously wounded, leaning on the other.

"*Ayeee.*" She pressed down on the accelerator.

I didn't have time to react.

Thump-thump.

Like two bags of flour dropped on pavement, one right after the other. The big RV slowed for an instant but kept on going. A tiny spray of blood dotted the bottom of the windshield.

She eased off the gas and turned the big rig in a wide arc, heading back to where it had been parked originally. After getting the nose pointed that way, she brought the RV to a stop and put the transmission into park.

She slumped in the seat, shoulders and arms shaking. After a few moments she turned and faced me, a few strands of hair dangling in front of impossibly green eyes. "What do you think of that, boyo?"

"Are you free this weekend?" I tried not to look at her cleavage. "Know a great Italian place in Dallas."

"Men. All the same." She pointed to my head. "Hey, you're bleeding."

I touched my temple and felt warm liquid oozing down my scalp.

"Here." She tossed me a paper napkin from Dunkin' Donuts.

"Thanks. What's your name?"

"What's it matter to you?"

"What do I call you?"

She sighed. "You won't be around long enough for that to be an issue, now, willya?"

Bria stuck her head into the driver's area, one hand on the back of each seat. "We need to get out of here."

"Gonna run again, are we?" the woman sitting next to me said.

"Shit, Colleen." Bria slapped the back of the driver's seat. "Patrick and Collin are both dead and there's blood on my baby."

"B-both of them are dead?" The woman sat upright in the driver's seat.

Bria pointed to me. "This one told me so."

"P-P-Patrick and Collin were my brothers." Colleen turned to me. Her eyes filled with tears, but she didn't cry.

"I'm sorry." I almost sounded like I meant it.

"I never trust you country folk."

"C'mon now." I tried for a little levity. "We're not all that bad."

"Really?" She pointed outside. "Then where are the police? Or the fire department?"

I didn't reply. She had a point. A firefight had just occurred on the outskirts of a midsized American city. Yet no sirens sounded in the distance. No helicopters from the local news team.

"It's true." Bria nodded. "Nobody looks after the Travelers but other Travelers."

Both women looked at me for a long few seconds. Finally, Colleen said, "And why exactly are you here?"

I told her what I had told Petey, which was the truth. A man was terrorizing a woman in Plano. Collin Toogoode was the one person who might ID him.

But he was dead, which meant I was back where I started. If you didn't count being stranded in a Winnebago with an ultra-hot, eminently doable Irish babe intent on ripping off my private parts while a crew of Fort Worth wiseguys were trying to kill us all.

I wished I hadn't smarted off to Felix and lost my job at the bar.

I wished I'd never met Olson.

I wished I'd paid attention in school so I could have gotten a real job.

"Look." Bria pointed to the front window. "It's Petey."

"Well, I'll be." Colleen tapped the horn twice. "And here I was thinking that he was really gonna leave this time."

Petey looked like he'd gone a couple of rounds with a methed-up bobcat. Or Colleen. His silk shirt was in tatters, there was a rip in the knee of his jeans, scratches on his face. Shoulders slumped, he carried the shotgun by the barrel with the butt dragging in the dirt.

"Hush, Colleen." Bria made a shushing sound. "Don't talk that way about your husband."

I looked at the blond woman. "Petey is your husband?"

She nodded. "Unfortunately so. For almost fifteen years."

"That's awfully young." I did some quick arithmetic. She couldn't have been over thirty, maybe thirty-two or -three tops.

"It was a good match, between our two families." Colleen crossed her arms. "And my father was a wealthy man. I came with a good dowry."

"This is true." Bria nodded, a knowing look on her face.

Petey had stopped about twenty feet in front of the Winnebago.

"A dowry?" I tried not to sound incredulous. "You two are aware that we're no longer living in the Middle Ages, right?"

Neither woman replied. The girl in the rear began to cry, and Bria turned and went back there.

Petey waved at us.

I motioned for him to come inside.

"What are you doing?" Colleen said.

"Trying to get the hell out of Dodge."

I heard the door open, so I got up and went to the back. Petey stood by the entrance. He was sweaty and dirty.

"What happened?" I said.

He shook his head but didn't reply, eyes wide and unblinking.

"Petey?" I took a step closer. "You okay?"

"He's probably drunk." Colleen appeared beside me.

"I killed him." Petey's voice was a whisper.

"Who?" I said.

"The man." He blinked several times. "The one who followed me."

"Troy Aikman?"

He nodded.

"Oh, for the love of God." Colleen stepped forward, blood rushing to her face. "You killed a fookin' football hero. There'll be no rest for any Traveler. They'll hunt us down like dogs."

Petey cowered like a man about to be hit. Based on the length of time I had known his wife, about seven minutes now, I could understand his trepidation.

"The guy was wearing a Troy Aikman jersey." I grabbed her arm and pulled her away from Petey. "It wasn't really him."

The RV was silent for a few moments. I looked at the leather sofa. Bria, her daughter, and the old woman were sitting there, huddled together. Bria stared at me, as if trying to say something with her eyes.

Petey broke the silence. "What about Collin?"

"He's dead," I said.

Bria wiped her eyes.

"We need to leave here," I said.

"We?" Colleen looked at me.

"Okay, you, then." I shrugged. "I'll get my car and leave you all to—"

"No, you're coming with us," Petey said. "You're not like the others."

"No country folk's riding in this trailer." Colleen crossed her arms.

"Yes, he is," Petey said quietly. His voice was an octave lower.

The air in the trailer seemed to get chilly as everyone quit speaking.

Even the child stopped crying and looked at the man and woman facing each other. I wondered about the chapters in their book up to this point. I wondered what it was like to live such a cloistered existence, keeping totally to yourself and your own, never trusting anyone but members of the clan. I wondered what it was like to have a clan.

"Look who's growing a set." Colleen smiled tightly. "All right, then, let's go."

CHAPTER THIRTY-TWO

Petey sat by his wife while she drove. Colleen said that there was a back way out of the compound and we'd leave through that exit, less chance of running into the bad guys. We'd get my borrowed VW later. If it was still there.

I plopped down on the captain's chair in the living area and stared at Bria and her daughter and the old woman.

The shadows were long across the fields of the Traveler compound as we motored toward the back of the acreage. We entered another small grove of live oaks, and the failing sunlight flashed across the inside of the Winnebago.

The burning RVs had begun to smolder now, the combustible material exhausted. I looked at my watch: 6:47 P.M. I was missing *The Simpsons*, yet another reason to detest my return to the life.

The little girl stared at me for a long time before speaking. "Where's my daddy?"

Bria made a tsking sound and smoothed her hair, a gesture identical to that of Anita Nazari as she had touched her daughter the day before.

I shook my head slowly, at a loss for what to say.

The old woman said something in the strange language and patted the girl on her shoulder. I assumed that the grandmother was blind or nearly, her eyes opaque like watery milk.

"Did Collin tell you anything before they got here?" I said to Bria.

"Not much. He was a mess, drunk and scared out of his wits," she said. "Couldn't say anything except how we were right, me and Patrick." She teared up again.

"What do you mean?" I sat forward. " 'We were right,' how?"

"Getting out of the traveling lif—"

The grandmother barked at the younger woman.

"Never mind." Bria shook her head. "I've said too much already."

The RV rattled over a cattle guard, disturbing a flock of grackles roosting in the trees. They took flight, a black sheet sluicing across the purple sky.

I looked at the three generations of Traveler women, huddled together on a tacky white sofa in a tricked-out recreational vehicle that cost more than most houses. Strangers in their own land was a cliché that didn't come close to properly describing them.

They lived here and had put down roots, evidenced by their property, but they didn't claim this place as their own. The road was home, wanderlust their curse or blessing, depending on your point of view.

I thought of arranged marriages in the age of Internet dating and what it must have been like to have the world at your fingertips yet not be able to partake of anything it had to offer. To be able to travel anywhere you wanted yet never be able to leave.

"You and your husband wanted out, didn't you?" I said to Bria.

She didn't reply, just stared at her lap, lips pursed.

"Nothing but trouble, you are." The old woman stood up, holding on to the side of the sofa for support, her milky eyes angry now. She pointed a bony finger at me. "Nothing comes from country folk but heartache and misery."

"What's going on back here?" Petey stumbled in from the cockpit area, bracing himself against the wall.

" 'Tis nothing at all, Petey." I put on my best Irish brogue. "Just talking to pass away the time."

He shot us a look, then retreated to the passenger's seat in the front. The old woman sat back down, muttering to herself. Bria scooped up her daughter and headed toward the back, where I assumed there was a bedroom. The RV rattled over another cattle guard and then onto asphalt, a two-lane farm-to-market road.

By the angle of the sun I could tell we were headed west and south, away from Weatherford, maybe toward Stephenville, or maybe just into the vastness of the middle part of Texas, narrow roads and small towns and endless miles of rocky soil and prickly hills trying hard to be mountains.

The Winnebago picked up speed. The ride evened out and became smoother. Petey appeared for a moment on his way to the rear of the trailer. He returned a few moments later with a chunk of corrugated cardboard and some duct tape. The wind whistling through the interior of the RV stopped as he covered the shattered window before going back to the front.

The old woman pointed her finger at me, motioning that I should join her on the sofa. I got up warily and walked over, sitting down a few feet from her.

She leaned toward me. "Collin told me something."

"What?"

"The man following him, he was the devil in the flesh." She crossed herself.

"I don't get it."

"He had the eyes of Satan."

I frowned, trying to understand. The old woman sat back and crossed her arms, nodding slowly as if she had just imparted the wisdom of the ages to me.

Bria came back into the living area, holding her daughter's hand. "Grandma Patty, leave Mr. Oswald alone now."

"I'll leave him alone when he tells me when my Sean is coming back." Patty banged the top of the sofa with one hand.

Sean? I moved back to the captain's chair. Who the hell was Sean?

"Oh, Grandma." Bria sat down beside the old woman and patted her hand. "You know that Grandpa Sean died ten years ago this past February."

"My Sean is dead?" The woman covered her mouth and began to weep.

Bria gave me a wan smile and rolled her eyes, a thanks-for-putting-up-with-my-senile-relative look. We drove on in silence, the twilight deepening. After another half hour the rig slowed and turned into the gravel parking lot of the Happy Cow Steakhouse, a worn-at-the-heels dump with wagon wheels lining the roof and a fake hitchin' post in front. The parking lot was full, pickups and big American four-door sedans, not a foreign car in sight.

I stood up. "What are we doing?"

"It's time to eat." Bria spoke matter-of-factly, as if everyone on the run from a crew of hired guns normally stopped at the Gristle Café for a leisurely meal.

"You're kidding, right?"

"The child needs food. We do, too," Bria said. "You and Petey can go. Get it for takeaway."

Petey appeared in the living area. "We're a long way from where we started, and we've been here before. It'll be all right."

I tried to ignore the rumbling in my stomach. I'd consumed nothing but a couple of ounces of Guinness in the past few hours.

Petey opened the door and looked at me. I swore and followed him outside into the cool of the early evening, our shoes crunching on gravel as we walked toward the entrance. The front door was decorated with horseshoes and lariats glued to the rough wood.

The inside was no better, decor like some third-rate Sizzler, over-weight waitresses with peroxided hair in too-tight denim uniforms.

I felt the stares as soon as we walked in but figured it for nothing but hey-look-at-the-city-slickers or maybe because of Petey's torn clothing.

Petey headed to the bar, where a TO GO sign hung over one corner and a small group of people sat on stools, working on beers and high-balls as a television at the far end flickered soundlessly.

The patrons at the bar were all white, various ages, and wore everything from starched khakis to faded jeans and T-shirts.

They were talking and laughing but stopped when we got there.

The bartender was a burly man with muttonchops and a greased-back pompadour high atop his skull. He looked at me and then at Petey and turned his back to us, spreading the sports page across the bar.

Petey picked up a menu sitting by the waitress station and opened it.

Nobody at the bar spoke; the clink of silverware and conversations coming from other parts of the restaurant sounded eerie in the vortex of silence that surrounded us. A handful of the people were staring into their drinks. The rest looked at us with flat expressions on their faces.

Petey closed the menu.

"Hey." I snapped my fingers and spoke to the bartender. "You want to take our order or what?"

"It's okay." Petey spoke quietly out of the corner of his mouth. "Give him a minute. He'll be around."

A man in his late forties was the closest person to us, sitting a couple of feet away, nursing a mug of draft beer. He wore a cream-colored felt Stetson, pressed khaki pants, and a white, Western-styled oxford cloth shirt with enough starch in it to stop a bullet.

"This's a respectable place we got here, you unnerstand?" His accent was thick and very nearly impenetrable to a passerby from either coast. "Mind your place, boy."

"My place?" I tried not to sound astounded. "What are you talking about?"

"Damn Gypsies." The man shook his head and took a long drink of beer.

"Don't take the bait," Petey whispered as he placed a hand on my shoulder. "Let it go."

Everybody at the bar was looking at us now. Nothing happened for about half a minute. Finally the bartender folded up the sports page, tossed it into the trash, and sauntered over to where we were standing.

"Y'all want to get something to go?" His voice was nasally, his tone condescending.

Petey nodded and smiled and ordered six cheeseburgers and fries and six unsweetened ice teas.

The bartender scribbled it all down and walked off without saying a word. Conversation slowly resumed.

Petey and I stood at the corner of the bar, a few feet away from Mr. Stetson. I felt his eyes on me but resisted looking at him. Five minutes stretched into ten.

"You got sumpin' you wanna say to me, boy?" He tilted his hat back a few inches and crossed his arms.

I stared at a spot on the bar and shook my head slowly. This was his territory, not mine.

Muttonchops arrived with the food. Petey paid the bartender with a crisp hundred-dollar bill, the light in the bar glinting on his gold Rolex as he handed the money over.

"Keep the change." He picked up the sack containing the food and turned to me. "Let's go."

Stetson drained his mug of beer and smiled as if he'd won something of great importance.

I tried to quell the cold anger that licked at my spine and made my arms feel tight and fingers ball into fists.

Stetson chuckled. "Think you're a tough guy, don'tcha?"

"We're leaving now, okay?" Petey pulled my arm. "No problems here."

"Right." I stepped away from the bar. "No problems."

Petey and I turned toward the front as Stetson pushed his bar stool back and got up. I heard him clopping behind us as we walked across the restaurant. I felt his eyes staring at my back.

We stepped through the doorway and out onto the rocky parking lot, the air smelling of gravel dust and mesquite smoke from the restaurant's fire pit.

Stetson followed us out.

I stopped, turned around.

Petey grabbed my arm. "No, this isn't the way."

"You sure there ain't sumpthin' you don't want to get off your chest, boy?" Stetson hooked his thumbs in his belt and stared at me. He was my height but about twenty pounds heavier, mostly in his gut. His hands were callused, fingers big as andouille sausages.

"Ever done it with a cow?" I said.

"Ohhh." Petey stared at the ground.

"What did you say?" Stetson frowned.

"A cow. You. Carnal knowledge." My smile was tight across my lips. "How about it?"

"You little piece of Gypsy trash." Stetson balled his fists. "You need to learn some respect, boy."

"You want, we can test the major medical portion of your HMO."

"Let's go." Petey pointed to the trailer at the far side of the parking lot. "We've got the food."

Stetson took a slow lumbering step my way, hands up like a boxer's. I went in fast and low, putting everything I had into one shot to his ample gut.

He sat down on the gravel, face flushed, a whooshing sound coming from his mouth and lips opened wide, searching for air.

"I think you owe me and my friend an apology." I backhanded him across the face, not a hard blow, meant more to humiliate than to do harm. His hat flew off and landed in the dust. "Now say you're sorry before I do some real damage."

He bobbled his head like a swimmer trying to get water out of his eyes.

"The country folk win this game." Petey pushed me away from the man. "They always have and always will."

I let him drag me toward the RV as Stetson sat on the gravel and tried to figure out what had just happened. Petey knocked on the door and Bria opened it. Once inside, he turned to me. "What the hell did you have to go and do that for, huh?"

"Do what?" Colleen said.

Petey explained what had happened. Everyone looked at me.

Bria said, "Are you daft, man?"

"Now we can't go back there." Colleen slapped her forehead.

"Why would you want to?" I said. "It's the twenty-first century, for God's sake. And they treat you like you're a second-class citizen."

"You still don't get it." Petey shook his head and laughed without humor. "We *are* second-class citizens."

CHAPTER THIRTY-THREE

Colleen drove west for another few miles before stopping at a state rest area, a wide paved spot on the side of the road with a small brick building housing restrooms next to a water fountain and a soft drink machine.

Several picnic areas lined the parking lot, concrete tables and benches sitting underneath a row of magnolia trees. Four or five eighteen-wheelers idled at the far end, amber safety lights glowing softly in the early evening air.

We stayed in the RV and ate, mostly in silence. I asked once how the people in the bar knew that Petey was a Traveler since he looked the same as they did.

"It's our way of life," he said. "They don't approve. Our means of earning a living doesn't meet the country folks' definition of acceptable, I guess."

That made no sense, but I didn't press it. After a few more minutes, Petey spoke again.

"They call us Gypsies, but we're not. That's the Roma, trash if you ask me. Pickpockets and shit."

A knock sounded at the door of the RV. I jumped up, moved to one side, and reached for the Benelli leaning against the wall.

Everyone else quit eating and looked at Petey. He opened a cabinet and said to me, "Don't worry, it's nothing." He answered the door and had a quick conversation with a man who was apparently a driver from one of the trucks parked down the way. He handed Petey some cash, and Petey slipped him a foil packet.

The door shut. Petey turned to me. "A little income on the side. You know, keeping the truckers awake. The road gets long sometimes."

I didn't say anything. Petey sat down and continued his dinner. A few minutes later everyone but me had finished eating. I realized that I didn't have much of an appetite anymore. I was no closer to finding the person or persons threatening Anita Nazari. The car I'd borrowed had probably been stolen, and I had no transportation except the RV of a bunch of professional ne'er-do-wells. Plus, I still had to track down Mike Baxter's daughter.

Bria cleared the dinner mess and disappeared into the back with her daughter and the old woman. Colleen and Petey got into a fight, over what I couldn't quite fathom. They swore at each other in the half-English, half-something-else hybrid. After a few minutes that passed, too, and Colleen pulled a bottle of white Zinfandel from the refrigerator in the galley area. She poured a large measure of pink wine into a baby blue frosted goblet, sat on the sofa, and drank half of it down in one gulp.

Petey turned to me. "Hope you don't mind sleeping on the sofa."

I awoke at dawn when the other passengers on the land yacht began to stir. I was tired, having slept fitfully, my slumber interrupted with dreams of angry men in Stetsons chasing me and visions of Colleen in a short nightgown, standing over me as I tossed and turned. I looked at the lipstick-stained wineglass on the table by the sofa and wondered where my reality intersected with another's irrationality.

After several hushed conversations on his cell phone, Petey got behind the wheel and drove toward Fort Worth. No stopping for breakfast on this trip. An hour later, he pulled to the side of the street leading into the Traveler compound in White Settlement.

He put the RV into park and walked into the living area. He pointed to the street. "Your car's down there."

"You sure?" I opened the door and stepped outside.

He nodded. "Best be forgetting this place, too."

Colleen stood by her husband. She stared at me with a blank look on her face.

"You can leave all this," I said. "Get a real job. And a life that doesn't involve selling speed to truckers and getting kicked out of crappy steak-houses."

"Go on. Get the hell out of here." He shut the door.

CHAPTER THIRTY-FOUR

Anita Nazari's VW sat where I had left it the day before, in one piece, all wheels attached, the ragtop undamaged.

I got in and looked at my watch: 7:35, Wednesday morning. I pulled out the slip of paper with Susan Baxter's address on it, did some calculations, and figured I had time for breakfast.

I drove to an IHOP near downtown where I had the Cardiologist's Special: bacon and eggs, hash browns, sausage patties, and a short stack of blueberry pancakes. And a pot of coffee I sweetened with some of that fake sugar stuff because, hey, everybody needs to watch their weight. I washed my face in the men's room and left.

The last location Mike had for his daughter had been her mother's home. The database search I'd conducted on Nolan's computer had turned up a different address, a house a few blocks off of the Texas Christian University campus, on a street obviously taken over by students, given the number of beer cans in yards and cars with TCU stickers.

I parked behind a Toyota Prius with a FREE TIBET sticker on the bumper, next to one for the Green Party. The car was directly in front of Susan's address, an older wood-frame structure badly in need of a fresh coat of paint.

The front yard was dirt and weeds and trash. A tombstone, stolen,

I hoped, leaned against the corner of a sofa that was to one side of the door.

A young man about twenty sat in the middle of the sofa. He was wearing cargo shorts, flip-flops, and a sleeveless T-shirt and reading a dog-eared copy of Norman Mailer's *The Armies of the Night,* pausing occasionally for sips of Bud Light from the bottle sitting in his lap.

He looked up when I was about ten feet away. He didn't say anything, just stared at me with that knowing, slightly smug look all twenty-year-olds have before they come to the realization that life is not one big Happy Meal waiting to be eaten at your leisure while the neverending keg of good times chills nearby.

"Hey," he said.

I pointed to the house. "Is this Susan Baxter's place?"

He frowned. I could see the thought processes working themselves out, the decision being made to act like something he wasn't. The shoulders squared, jaw tightened, eyes narrowed. I imagined there had probably been a De Niro film festival on AMC last night, or a Dirty Harry flick, something to account for the faux toughness.

"Who wants to know?" He wedged his beer between two cushions and stood up.

"Me." I spoke softly.

"Yeah?" He crossed his arms. "And just who the hell are you?" His voice cracked a hair.

Very slowly I walked toward him until we were face-to-face, a few inches separating our noses.

He crossed his arms and swallowed repeatedly as if his throat were dry.

I placed the palm of my right hand on his chest and pushed.

He fell backward onto the sofa, dislodging the beer, causing it to spill on his copy of *The Armies of the Night.*

"Shit." He picked up the paperback and thumbed the pages, droplets of beer misting across the sofa. "You ruined my book."

"I'm a friend of Susan's father's," I said. "Is this her house?"

He stopped trying to dry the wet pages and looked up at me.

"I'm not here to mess up anything you or she's got going," I said. "Just want to talk with her for a couple of minutes."

"I think she's awake now. We had kind of a late night." He set the book on the back of the sofa, opened to the spot he'd been reading. "How do I know you're really a friend of her father's? She never even talks about him."

"You don't. Stay out here, okay?" I walked to the front of the house and pushed open the door.

A two-foot square of tile formed the entryway, like an island in the sea of dirty carpeting that covered the floor of the tiny living room. The air held the faint traces of marijuana smoke and a trash can long overdue for emptying.

On one wall was another sofa, in marginally better shape than the one outside. The coffee table was an old door on cinder blocks, littered with empty beer bottles, overflowing ashtrays, half a dozen or so books, and a bong.

A girl carrying a bowl of cereal and wearing a pair of denim shorts and a Che Guevera T-shirt came out of the kitchen. Her hair was pinned on top of her head, one strand dangling in front of puffy eyes. The jawline and high, wide cheekbones were familiar; I knew I had found Mike Baxter's daughter.

"Who are you?" She shoveled a spoonful of cereal into her mouth.

"Your father hired me to track you down."

Crunch, crunch.

"He wants to talk to you."

"How is dear old Dad?" Her words were muffled because of the cereal.

"He's sick. Pretty bad, sounds like."

Susan Baxter put the bowl down on the coffee table next to a hardback book titled *A History of American Genocide* and a Danielle Steel paperback.

"Fuck him," she said.

"Nice thing to say about the only dad you've got."

"You have no clue about anything."

I nodded slowly. "That's true on most days, I'll give you that."

"He hires some rent-a-pig out of the Yellow Pages and thinks that will fix every—"

"We're old friends. I remember seeing you when you were in grade school."

She raised one eyebrow.

"Your dad and I served together in the first Gulf War."

"Oh, I see." She nodded with great exaggeration, a smug look on her face. "Another killing machine we've got here."

"He wants to make peace with you."

"So did you come back all screwed up, too, because the Pentagon lied?" She stuck her chin out.

"I don't follow."

"The vaccines they gave you, supposed to be harmless." She laughed. "That's a joke. I could show you the Web sites, the people that have died. You cannot believe how evil our government is."

"He loves you very much," I said.

"First Christmas he's back, I'm, like, five." She paused for a moment, emotion ragged in her voice. "He's got these headaches and sores on his body and the VA says it's all in his head. So he gets drunk and throws our TV through the window and then locks my mom in the closet."

"I didn't know." I tried not to look around at the dirty house. I felt guilty for my own good health.

"T-t-try growing up with that, see if you want to have a big reunion anytime soon."

I watched a roach crawl across the wall.

"All for some oil for the imperialist war machine." She picked up the bowl of cereal but put it down a second later and shook a cigarette out of a pack of American Spirits sitting by the bong.

"I'm gonna leave my cell number." I grabbed a pad and pen from the mess on the coffee table. "And your dad's room number at the VA in Dallas."

"War is horrible, like a cancer on society." She put the cigarette in her mouth but didn't light it.

"Preaching to the choir." I dropped the pad back on the table. "He's gonna die soon. Like any day now."

Susan Baxter lit her cigarette and blew a plume of smoke over the coffee table.

"He goes without you two talking, you'll regret that the rest of your life."

"Get out." Tears welled in her eyes.

I left, softly shutting the door behind me. The guy who'd been reading the book stood in the front yard, watching me.

"You give a damn about her?" I said. "Or you just laying some pipe?"

"She's my girlfriend," he said. "We're gonna join the Peace Corps together."

"Then go in there and be nice, because she needs somebody about now." I brushed past him, headed toward the VW.

"What'd you do to her?" he shouted after me.

I stopped by the driver's door. "Tried to make a difference."

CHAPTER THIRTY-FIVE

The traffic on the turnpike between Dallas and Fort Worth slowed to a crawl near the exit for Lone Star Park, the horse track and pari-mutuel betting mecca in Grand Prairie, on the western fringes of Dallas County.

I cranked the AC on high and watched exhaust shimmer through the air.

The midmorning sun looked like an egg yolk swimming in a pool of Crisco, and the Dallas skyline was barely visible only a few miles ahead, the rugged concrete-and-glass mountain range gossamer from the pollution.

Traffic inched along, the road narrowing near the Sylvan Avenue exit as yet another construction crew worked on the blacktop, enlarging this, rerouting that.

To the right lay Oak Cliff, one quadrant of the southern section of Dallas, an older part of town full of rolling hills and narrow streets lined with prewar bungalows and residents looking for cheap housing or a slower-paced lifestyle. To the left lay mile after mile of warehouses, stretching from the turnpike up to the Trinity River.

Another few hundred yards inched by. My cell phone rang.

"Yell-lo."

"You are not a very conscientious employee, are you?" Anita Nazari's voice sounded hollow on the other end of the line. She was going for angry but only managed petulant.

"I'm not your employee."

"You took my money."

A man behind me in an extended cab Ford pickup honked. I looked up. The traffic jam had broken.

"Why haven't you checked in?" she said. "It's been almost forty-eight hours."

"Your guy's been keeping me busy." I decided that, while on the cell phone, it would be best not to get into the carnage that had occurred over the course of the last day or so.

"*My guy*?" The anger in her voice was unmistakable. "Are you referring to the madman who has been stalking me and my daughter for over two years? Is that who you are calling 'My Guy'?"

"Yep. That's the one."

Frosty silence.

"He's a pro, a seriously bad cat." The skyline grew clearer the closer the VW got to downtown. "Might be time to take a little vacation."

"I am a researcher. I have projects, a staff to consider." She spoke slowly, as if addressing a child. "I cannot just leave. That's why I hired you, remember?" She said the last as if she was speaking to a *slow-witted* child.

"Maybe call the police, then." I tried to calm my anger.

"The authorities fill out forms, type things up." Her voice grew quiet. "Or they put you on a list."

I didn't reply as I drove across the Trinity River, the full unblemished view of downtown now clearly visible in all its phallic glory.

The turnpike ended and offered several choices. Take Interstate 35 north and head to my motel room for a shower and a change of clothes. Take the interstate south and visit Mike Baxter at the VA. Tell him about his daughter, maybe put a good spin on the meeting, if that was possible.

"I didn't realize you were a quitter," Anita said.

"I'm not." I thought about Ari's Social Club, the next likely place to learn about her stalker.

"Let's see . . . you told me you got fired from your last job, and now you're quitting this one."

I clenched the steering wheel until my knuckles were white but didn't say anything.

"I need you to come to my house in Plano." She paused. "There have been some developments."

"What are you talking about?" I headed north on Interstate 35, past the bulbous Reunion Tower and the American Airlines Center. I could take the Dallas North Tollway and head to her house.

"Where are you right now?" she asked.

"Downtown Dallas. Tell me wha—"

"I will see you in thirty minutes, then." The line went dead.

CHAPTER THIRTY-SIX

One hour later I parked in front of Anita Nazari's house behind an elderly pickup truck full of lawn equipment. The Range Rover sat in the driveway.

I was late.

I'd stopped at a bookstore on Park at Preston, a few minutes away from Anita's place. I'd bought a cup of coffee and the *Dallas Morning News*. Got caffeinated and caught up on current events. Then I had leafed through a copy of the glossy enquirer, *People* magazine, and learned the latest happenings among the one-named beautiful people, Britney and Brad and Angelina and the rest of the Hollywood crowd.

Call it a little "me time." Call it I-don't-like-to-get-bossed-around. Call it whatever you want, no way was I showing up on her schedule.

After I'd finished with the coffee and magazine, I'd driven to the suburban Mediterranean-style house that Anita Nazari called home.

A Hispanic man stood in the front yard, emptying a lawn-mower sack full of clippings into a plastic garbage bag. He smiled and nodded hello as I walked up the sidewalk. The air smelled like fresh-cut grass and gasoline exhaust.

My back ached from sleeping on the narrow sofa in the Winnebago. I was dirty and tired and pissed off.

I rang the bell.

Anita Nazari opened the door. She wore a white terry-cloth robe that stopped midthigh. The robe was cinched at the waist, exposing cleavage encased in a yellow bikini top. Her hair was wet, kept out of her eyes by a pair of sunglasses perched on the top of her head.

"I'm sorry about what I said on the phone," she said.

I stared at her.

"I'm under a lot of pressure. From this man . . . and work."

"So you took a mental health day?" I nodded at her clothing.

"The cable people came earlier. I decided to take the morning off. Maybe the afternoon, too." She shifted her weight, and the robe came open another notch. "Please come in. I am truly sorry for my attitude earlier." She moved to one side of the entrance, and I stepped inside.

The house was quiet. She shut the door behind me as the lawn mower started up. Just another morning in suburbia.

"Would you like something to drink?" She headed toward the kitchen, the back of her thighs a captivating sight underneath the short robe.

"You said there was a new development?" I followed her into the rear of the house.

She didn't reply or stop at the kitchen. Instead she glanced over her shoulder once, a strand of damp hair dangling in front of her eyes. She opened the sliding glass door leading to the patio and stepped outside. I did the same.

The patio was flagstone, covered by an overhang from the house. Outdoor speakers played music softly, the Dixie Chicks singing about wide open spaces.

A built-in outdoor fireplace was to the left, an expensive-looking gas grill to the right. In the middle was a glass-topped table and chairs. A ceiling fan swirled overhead, keeping the shaded area relatively cool.

Anita slipped off the robe and dropped it onto a chair, her skin glistening with oil. She tossed her sunglasses onto the table next to a pager and a cell phone before heading to the pool.

"Stop," I said.

She stopped.

"Why am I here?"

"I need someone to protect me." She turned to face me. "Why is that so hard to understand?"

"You hired me to investigate the guy who was threatening you."

"And I don't like quitters, either," she said. "You're not a quitter, are you, Hank Oswald?"

"No. But I've investigated, and my advice is to call the police."

She turned, walked the few remaining feet to the pool, and dove in. Her body sliced through the water like a tan shark. She shot to the other end of the pool without coming up for air, did a flip turn while still underwater, and kicked her way to the middle before surfacing.

The pool was not deep at that point, coming only to where her legs connected to her torso, a stretch of light brown skin bisected by the yellow bikini bottom. Water sluiced down her chest and abdomen, sparkling in the sun like a thousand carats of molten diamonds.

I could smell the dried sweat on my body mixed with the greasy aroma of the IHOP from earlier that morning. Felt the texture of day-old, slept-in clothes. I imagined myself back at the Studio Six, taking a long, hot shower before getting fresh jeans and a clean shirt.

The music changed, another Dixie Chicks tune, this one about missed opportunities and "a home that might have been," the lyrics all the more plaintive because of Natalie Maines's remarkable voice.

Anita let herself fall backward into the sparkling water, drifting languidly toward the far end of the pool.

"There haven't been any new developments, have there?" I stretched my neck, working a kink out.

Anita rolled over and swam to my end of the pool. She stood up, the water coming to her knees now. "You and I are much the same, you know."

"I seriously doubt that." I tried to look at her face, not the rivulets of water tracing paths across her flawless skin.

"Outsiders, looking in." She scratched the inside of one thigh. "I could see it in your eyes the first time we met."

"I've checked you out. You never stay in one town for very long."

"There's safety in movement. I learned that early on," she said. "Old habits die hard."

"Why is this guy after you?"

She walked up the steps leading out of the pool, stopping when we were a few inches apart. "Do you ever get lonely, even in a city as large as Dallas?"

"I'm a burnt-out and barely employed private investigator who lives in an extended-stay motel." I could smell her skin now, chlorine, sweat, tanning lotion. "You tell me how lonely I get."

"I try to talk to Tom about all this . . ." She shook her head slightly. "But his world revolves around football matches and beer with his buddies after work."

"Tom's a man of simple tastes." I kept my eyes focused on her face instead of her cleavage. "So why do you hang out with him?"

"He's a kind and decent person." She crossed her arms under her breasts. "Unfortunately, nice people don't understand the dark side of human nature."

I nodded but couldn't think of anything pertinent to add to her simple statement of fact.

"Tom doesn't make me feel safe." She stared at the ground, eyes vacant, going to a dark crevice on the outer fringes of her consciousness, the point in time when things went from good to bad, a sliver of her soul I could never get to in a thousand years of trying.

"Real safety is an . . . illusion." My voice grew hoarse as I tried to control my breathing. I always wanted to go to that shadowy spot in a woman's soul. I was a fixer, a righter of wrongs, and it galled me to think I couldn't smooth the wrinkles of her existence and make it all better. "The best we can hope to do is keep the barbarians at the gate one day at a time."

"I'm sorry to get you involved. You didn't even want to get messed up with me, my problems, anyway," she said. "I-I'll call the police."

I didn't reply, trying to ease my breathing. My head felt light, dizzy.

She kissed me on the lips, her hand sliding up my arm to the back of my head.

I pressed my lips to hers for a moment and then pushed her away. "Sorry."

"You're right. This isn't the time or the place." She crossed her arms under her breasts again and hugged herself.

"Last time I got involved with a client it turned out badly for everybody."

She nodded and returned her gaze to the ground.

I cleared my throat. "The bad guy's taken out the only witness." I decided to get back to business and tried not to stare at her breasts, now even more prominent with her arms pushing them up. "He's pretty connected, seems like."

"What other avenues of investigation are left, then?" She walked around me and grabbed her robe.

"I have a slim lead." I followed her inside, remembering Fedora's mention of Ari the Dallas mobster. "It's tough to not leave *any* trail."

"Then pursue it." She pulled a container of orange juice from the refrigerator.

"I thought you were going to call the police."

"You think they'll help?" She poured a glass of juice without offering me any. "Or even understand?"

"You keep changing your mind; gives me a headache," I said. "I'm going back to my place and clean up a little."

"Wait." She disappeared through a small door by the refrigerator.

A few moments later she emerged carrying a Nordstrom shopping bag. "You're registered under your own name at the motel?"

"Yeah."

"Maybe you should clean up and change here." She pointed to the far side of the family room. "There's a full bath in there."

She had a point, but I didn't want to admit it.

"What's that?" I pointed to the bag.

"I bought Tom some clothes the other day. No particular reason. But I think they might be more useful if you took them and didn't go back to your motel for a while."

I debated the choice for a moment and then took the sack and headed to the bathroom. The shower felt great, and the clothes, a black ribbed T-shirt and designer jeans, though not my style, fit pretty well, including the Cole Haan loafers.

Ten minutes later I emerged in a cloud of steam, hair damp, ready to head to Ari's.

Anita was standing in the hallway, still wearing the robe.

"I expect to be kept posted this time," she said. "I want to know of your activities."

"If your phone's not ringing, it's me." I walked out of her house and headed to Dallas.

CHAPTER THIRTY-SEVEN

The Professor increased the flow from the tank by a few milliliters, feeling the pure oxygen fill his lungs. He looked at the IV bag hanging from a hook on his closet door. It was three-quarters empty, nearly ten grams of pure vitamin C coursing through his veins now, binding with the poisons there, cleansing his system.

He'd upped his dose of magnesium, too, until he felt his bowels rumble and knew he'd reached his tolerance. Any more would do little good combating the insecticide he'd ingested.

He wished he'd been able to draw out the experience of dying for the Gypsy, but that wouldn't have been the act of a professional.

He smiled and closed his eyes. Felt the pains in his thoracic cavity lessen a fraction as the antioxidants did their work. The second contractor was dead. The mission secure. The drip of the IV and the hiss of the oxygen tank were soothing, restful.

The buzzing startled him. He opened his eyes, and looked from side to side as he sat up, trying to remember where he was.

Dallas. The rented room. The IV bag still had a quarter to go. He must have dozed off for a moment.

The buzz sounded again. The cell phone they'd given him, only for use in emergencies. He looked at his watch. Noon Wednesday, the next check-in not due for another day.

He yanked off the oxygen mask. The phone was in a small black bag in the corner. He got off the bed and lost his balance, falling to the floor.

The IV ripped from the vein in the crook of his elbow. Blood dribbled down his forearm. He found a discarded alcohol wipe next to the bed and stuck it on the wound, folding his arm to hold it in place.

Buzz.

He crawled to the bag and unzipped it one-handed, flipping open the Motorola. "Yes?"

Silence like in a long, empty hall, electronic echoes, faint crackling. Then a man's voice said, "Hold one moment, please."

The Professor leaned against the wall and stared at his spattered blood on the floor, a forensics nightmare if it ever came to that. After what seemed like an eternity, the voice of his employer came on the line.

"You were hired to do a job, weren't you, sugar?" Her voice contained a mild rebuke hidden under the usual languid drawl.

"Are you not satisfied with my performance?" The Professor moved the phone from his mouth for a moment and cleared phlegm from his throat. "You called me off, remember?"

"You were supposed to take care of this doctor and her research days ago." The woman's voice on the other end of the line sounded angry now. "To end her threats and what they represented to our people."

"You don't know what it's like in the field."

"I know you were told to stay away from her until things were clear and you ignored a goddamn direct order."

He didn't reply. She had never sworn before. He wondered for a moment how they'd known about his breach of orders, but the question didn't linger in his mind very long. They always knew. They were in the knowing business.

"Procedures. Goddam procedures. Now I have to fill out a form."

The woman's voice had lost all traces of southern charm, sounding now like the GS-14 the Professor imagined her to be. "I hate to fill out forms. A fucking paper trail for this type of thing. Can you imagine?"

He shut his eyes. "You've really left me no choice."

"The situation is under control."

"Please." The use of the word pained him. Begging now. He had no other option. Even with his reputation, the offers were precious few these days for a man with his skills.

"A rogue. Never would have believed it." The woman laughed.

"No." The Professor felt his face blanch. The implications of her words stunned him. The vast network of agents at her disposal, now coming after him. "Y-you don't understand."

"Oh, sugar. You used to be the best."

"Everything is in place." The Professor stood up, trying to project his voice as stronger. "The assignment will be executed as ordered. You're not a field operative; these things take time to do properly."

"As much as you want, you can't turn the clock back." The drawl in the woman's voice had returned, but she sounded distracted now.

"Fine." The Professor managed to get a sense of outrage into his voice. "I'll take care of the job right now."

He listened for a reply, but there was none. The phone was dead.

CHAPTER THIRTY-EIGHT

Anita Nazari sat behind her desk at the administration building and stared at the Starbucks latte cooling on her blotter, next to the picture of Mira as a baby nestled in the arms of her father. The picture had been taken six months before his final trip to Afghanistan, almost ten years ago, three months before the divorce was final.

A classified mission gone bad, according to the man in the charcoal gray suit who had visited her at Johns Hopkins, where she had been serving her internship at the time. The man in the suit had eyes that never blinked and reminded her of a Savak agent, a member of the shah's secret police, tense and arrogant at the same time.

A stack of files and correspondence needing her attention sat on one side of her desk, a Dell desktop with twenty or more unanswered e-mails on the other.

She ignored both and sipped coffee, thinking about the man named Lee Oswald, wondering where he was, what he had learned, if anything.

Her assistant, a thin young man named Dave, entered her office without knocking, a manila folder under his arm. Dave bleached his hair until it was the color of straw and wore a small gold hoop in each earlobe. Anita wondered if he did these things to annoy her.

"This needs your signature." He put the file on her desk by the picture of Mira.

"Thank you."

"You want me to wait?"

Anita stared at the insipid young man but didn't reply.

"It's almost the end of the quarter, you know." Dave tugged on an earring. "Administration wants everything in on time."

"We mustn't keep the administration waiting." Anita picked up the stack of papers and signed the three top pages where Dave had left yellow Post-it notes indicating the proper line. Signing right now didn't matter anyway. The result had been transmitted earlier in the day. This was just a formality, and the final report would need her signature yet again.

"Now leave." She tossed him the file, a few errant papers sliding out and hitting the floor.

Dave looked like he was going to say something, a smart retort, no doubt, but apparently changed his mind. He shook his head slowly, picked up the loose pages, and left.

Anita spun around in her chair and stared out the seventh-floor window behind her desk. Her office overlooked downtown Dallas, the skyline smudged with ozone and smog.

The administration wouldn't particularly care one way or the other about her latest project. Her efforts were not directed toward the glamour research areas such as AIDS or breast cancer, or to topics that might lead to a patentable drug—the money shot of medical research, to use the crass vernacular of some of her male colleagues.

In fact, her latest effort was even more obscure than usual, merely proving that a certain substance was evident in the blood of veterans suffering from the so-called Gulf War Syndrome. She doubted the work would even get published, another factor sure to anger her superiors.

She was used to angering people. It provided a buffer of sorts she found comforting. The more she considered her tenuous position at the med school in Dallas, as well as the continued threats, the more she realized it was time to move again. At a conference last year she had met the head of recruiting for UCLA. She tried to remember where she had left his card.

CHAPTER THIRTY-NINE

Ari's Social Club, watering hole for much of the criminal element in Dallas, was on Samuell Boulevard on the east side of town, a few blocks from Interstate 30. The bar sat in the middle of a worn-out strip center, between a fried chicken joint called the Crispy Clucker and a liquor store with iron burglar bars in the windows. Across the street was a topless bar and a decrepit motor hotel so ancient it looked like a set piece from the *Perry Mason* show.

I pulled the VW into the parking lot, past a couple of tired-looking streetwalkers wearing fishnet hose and sports bras, and a skinny guy sitting on the curb in a long-sleeved shirt, sniffing and shaking and talking to himself.

The front door to Ari's Social Club, portal to a world I never imagined seeing again, taunted me. I closed my eyes for a few moments, hoping it would go away. Unfortunately the bar remained in place, much as the earth continued to turn, and bad guys kept being bad.

I stepped inside. Nothing had changed. A bar on the far right wall, tables clustered in the center, pool tables on the opposite side. Sports memorabilia dotted the walls: signed pictures of long-retired Dallas Cowboys and a framed poster from their first Super Bowl win in 1972. There was a story attached to that world championship, something about Ari not laying off enough action and a group from Miami being none too happy about it. Details were sketchy. A guy from Florida getting his hands chopped off. One of Ari's goons ending up a floater in the Trinity River.

A handful of people were sitting at the tables, watching ESPN on the big screen by the door leading to the back. I recognized a few of them. Two pimps. A bookie from South Dallas. A strip club owner and his main squeeze, a call girl I used to see a lot at one of the downtown hotels.

One of the pimps nodded hello as I walked toward the bar.

Stinky Larry Delgado, the manager of Ari's, stood behind the beer taps, drinking seltzer water.

Stinky Larry suffered from hyperhidrosis, or uncontrollable sweating. Didn't matter the weather, the dead of summer or a January blizzard, Stink oozed sweat like a union scab at a Teamsters' beer bust, leaving a puddle if he stood still for very long. He covered the stench ineffectively with off-brand cologne that smelled sort of like spoiled fruit.

"Heya, Stink." I sat down on a stool by the beer taps. "How's it hanging?"

"As I live and breathe, the Kennedy killer is in the house." Stinky Larry mopped his dripping brow with a bar towel. "Heard you were out of the life."

"You heard right." I leaned away from the bar for a moment as an invisible cloud of Larry funk drifted my way.

"Just dropping in here at the Ritz to shoot the breeze about old times?" Stink drank some more seltzer. The armpits of his baby blue oxford shirt were navy with perspiration, matching the half-moon slices of moisture underneath his flabby pectoral muscles.

"Ari here?"

"Who wants to know?" Stinky Larry frowned, looking serious.

"Uhh . . . me." I looked around the bar to see who else might be asking.

"Not a good time, Hank." He leaned across the counter, motioning me closer for a tête-à-tête. "Gee's in the house."

"Who?" I suppressed my gag reflex as much as possible. Up close, Stinky Larry smelled like a thousand sweaty jockstraps lying on a brothel floor.

"The Effe." Larry leaned away, raised one eyebrow, and nodded knowingly. "Getting their freak on."

"Not following you, Stink." I remembered now that Larry, despite being a pudgy, sweating white guy in his late fifties, liked to think of himself as hip and trendy and urban, all down with the gangstas and stuff. Unfortunately, he was usually a few years behind the times and rarely used the lingo correctly.

"Shizzle." He rolled his eyes.

"The Gee and the Effe." I scratched my head. "That some new rap band?"

One of the pimps sauntered up to the bar, an empty beer pitcher in his hand. Stinky Larry dribbled his way over and filled the container with Bud Light. When he returned he said, "Time off from the street make you all stupid or what?"

I sighed. "A moment of His Excellency's time, I beseech you. I pray to ask his indulgence in releasing a modicum of information."

"The hell you talking about, homey?" Stinky Larry frowned and a fresh sheet of perspiration dappled his face.

"Ari. Me. Talkie-talkie."

Stinky Larry leaned across the bar all the way, the stench unbearable now. He looked both ways and then said, "The Man. Is here. *Capische?*"

I held my breath, willing the smell away as Stink's gobbledygook began to make sense.

The Effe, the Gee. Federal. G-Man.

Federal agents. At Ari's Social Club, a virtually unheard-of occurrence. Ari was as crooked as a vice cop with three ex-wives and a dime-a-day coke habit, yet he prided himself on avoiding scrutiny from the Feds.

No guns, no drugs, no money laundering. Nothing that might trigger a federal eye being cast his way. Merely old-school stuff: prostitutes, gambling, loan sharking, that sort of thing.

I had started to say something when the bell over the front door jangled.

Larry and I turned.

The midafternoon sun sent shafts of light through the smoky bar as a sea of men in navy blue fatigues coursed through the narrow opening like dark water rushing through a canyon.

They wore flak jackets and carried MP5 submachine guns, pistols strapped to thighs, extra magazines in nylon pouches Velcroed to their vests. One man turned around to check the far corners of the bar, the yellow stenciling on the back of his jacket clearly visible from across the room.

F-B-I.

No one spoke. Not the patrons of the bar nor the agents. The sound on the big screen was off, no music playing on the jukebox. No noise at all in what had been a lively place only a few seconds before.

The agents fanned out, not drawing down on anybody, their weapons pointed downward at a forty-five-degree angle where they could be brought to bear in an instant.

All of the patrons were extremely still, most no doubt wondering how to ditch whatever illegal substances and/or weapons they were carrying. I didn't move either, but not out of fear. I had nothing illegal on me, nor was I wanted for anything.

The front part of Ari's was one big room, and it didn't take them long to determine no immediate threat existed. I counted eight agents. No one person appeared to be in charge, though they functioned as if they'd rehearsed securing Ari's Social Club a hundred times.

One agent spoke into a microphone clipped to his lapel.

The door to the back rooms opened and Ari appeared, a cigar in his mouth, standing immediately in front of a taller man in a dark gray suit and with close-cropped hair.

Ari had the lifts in, so he was nearing five feet tall. He wore a pair of dark slacks and an untucked yellow-and-lavender-patterned silk shirt so obnoxiously bright it hurt the eyes to look at for too long. He could have been an extra on *The Sopranos* if they ever staged an all-midget production.

Ari looked around the room before his eyes settled on me. He swaggered to the bar where I was standing, the man in the suit trailing behind him.

"That's him." Ari pointed a stubby finger at me. "That's Lee Oswald."

CHAPTER FORTY

The guy in the suit stepped around Ari, a pair of cuffs dangling from his hand.

One of the fatigue-clad agents slung his machine gun over his shoulder and approached me. "Hands on your head."

"What the hell?" I held my palms up and looked at the stubby wiseguy. "Ari, I haven't been in here for a year. What are you busting my chops for?"

"Book him, Danno." Ari grinned and rolled the cigar from one side of his mouth to the other.

The suit and the agent came at me from different directions. The suit said, "We can do this the hard way or the easy way."

I put my hands on my head and let them do it the easy way. Suit grabbed my left wrist. Agent grabbed the right. They flipped me around so that I faced the bar. Pulled my hands behind my back at the same time they pushed me over the bar. My face squished down on top of Stinky Larry's sweat rag.

"*Arrrgh.*" My revulsion at the grotesque stench was overwhelmed by the slimy feel of the cloth against my face. Click-click went the cuffs, cold steel on my wrists. Hands grabbed my elbows and pulled me away from the bar, the smoky air seeming as fresh as the wind roaring through a mountain pass in the Rockies.

"Lee Oswald?" Suit stood in front of me, hands on his hips. He was in his midthirties, but the look in his eyes and the way he carried himself were as old as death itself. He was a warrior, a Roman centurion or one of Rommel's tank commanders if he'd been born in a different time.

"Yeah." I nodded. "Thought we'd already established that."

"I have some questions."

"Me, too." I tried to look tough, but that didn't work well with the handcuffs. "I'll go first. Who the hell are you?"

Ari snorted. The rest of the patrons of the bar sat silently watching the drama unfold.

"Special Agent John Jordan." The suit flipped open a wallet, displaying a badge and photo with the seal of the Federal Bureau of Investigation partially embossed across the agent's face.

"You get the decoder ring to go with that?"

"It's like the handcuffs." Jordan cocked his head to one side. "We can do this the hard way or the easy way."

"I got nothing you want."

Jordan squinted and stared at me as if I were the zoo's newest chimp, his expression one of mild curiosity overshadowed by the unshakable fact that he was the higher-functioning primate despite our common DNA structure.

"What's with the handcuffs anyway?" I said. "Not like I've done anything wrong."

No reply.

"I want to talk to a lawyer," I said.

Jordan nodded slowly, as if he were pondering it. Then he turned and faced the people watching us. "During the course of our investigation, a person of interest, to wit one Lee Henry Oswald, has refused to answer our questions."

"Don't you dare." I kept my voice low as a trickle of sweat meandered down the small of my back.

"Because of Lee Henry Oswald's refusal to cooperate"—he turned and looked at me when he said my name—"we will have to conduct interviews and search each of you."

"You little piece of monkey shit." Ari hopped up and down, pointing his cigar at me. "Worm food is what you're gonna be."

One of the pimps muttered something under his breath. The bookie banged the table.

Jordan kept going. "We have officers from the Dallas vice squad standing by—"

"You win," I said softly.

Jordan turned. His face was still impassive, but there was a tiny gleam of triumph in his eyes. He spoke to the agent in the blue fatigues standing by my side. "In the back."

The agent pushed me toward the door leading to the rear rooms of Ari's Social Club, Jordan following. We were in a long hallway. To the right was a small open area that served as Ari's office, complete with a desk, a safe, and enough closed-circuit TV monitors to keep tabs on a casino.

The hall stopped at a room about the size of a large suburban den. On one side was a craps table, on the other a blackjack setup. The walls had been painted red. A broken pool cue lay on the floor next to a spent twelve-gauge shotgun shell and a chewed cigar butt.

The uniformed agent pushed me into a chair by a jukebox.

Jordan flipped another chair around and sat facing me with the back between his legs, forearms resting on the top.

"Good thing the vice cops aren't back here." I looked around at all the gaming equipment.

Jordan didn't reply.

"You ever see *Casablanca,* when Claude Rains tells Bogie how shocked he is to see gambling going on in his place?"

Jordan scratched his cheek once but didn't say anything.

"Were you born without a personality or did you have it surgically removed when you joined J. Edgar's outfit?"

"Do you know this person?" He pulled a five-by-seven photograph from his breast pocket and held it in front of my face. The photo was a portrait of a man in his early to middle thirties, close-cropped, sandy blond hair, wearing desert camo BDUs and a green beret with the distinctive insignia on the crown indicating he was a member of the special forces.

The background reminded me of my own formal picture taken before I had shipped out almost twenty years before.

"That's from Desert Storm, right?" I said.

Jordan nodded.

"I don't recognize him. Got anything more recent?"

"Sorry." The agent shook his head. "Newer stuff is not available to anybody without a security clearance."

"What's the guy's name?"

Jordan smiled tightly and shook his head. He turned and nodded at the uniformed fed, indicating for him to leave. The agent did.

"Uh . . . what's he done?" I wasn't all that happy to be alone with the man.

"You went on a raid, late January 1991 I think it was."

I shrugged. "That was a long time ago."

"You and your best friend, a former Cowboy named Olson and two other guys from your Ranger squad." He drummed his thumbs on the back of the chair. "You hit a villa in-country pretty far, way into Iraqi territory at the time."

"You've got some good security clearance mojo yourself." I nodded.

"It was a spook operation," Jordan said. "A colonel in the Republican Guard, one of Saddam's cousins, guy with high intel value. He'd turned the villa into his own private brothel. Lightly guarded."

I didn't say anything. The operation had been classified, so far off the books that something really messy must be going on if an FBI agent sixteen years later knew the details.

"The point is that you're not a stranger to the way things work," he said.

"What do you want from me?"

"It gets dirty sometimes." Jordan sighed and rubbed his eyes, indicating for the first time that he was not a robot. "Circumstances often require things to be done in a certain way, that, you know, might not be all that . . . traditional."

"Or legal?" I said.

"It's like making sausage. People would rather not know."

"When do you tell me this is a matter of national security?" I smiled. "Don't want to miss that part."

"When an operative goes native, he doesn't have an infrastructure anymore." Jordan stood up and wandered to the craps table. He picked up a pair of dice and tossed them against the padded side. "You understand what I'm saying?"

"Where do I fit in with your missing army man?" I remembered the hired Fort Worth muscle used to take down the Traveler camp.

"You've had contact with him."

I didn't say anything.

"The NSA *occasionally* lets us in on things that hit their information grid." He crossed the room to the blackjack table, picked up a stack of chips.

An image of Nolan's stepson, Max, flashed through my mind.

"They've got technology the rest of us can't even conceive of." He tossed a chip across the room. It landed on the craps table. "You think some half-ass hacker starts digging around, it doesn't get noticed?"

I stared at the craps table, making my face as impassive as possible. Connecting me to the hacking attempt would be difficult.

"Plus, the Weatherford police department found a gun with your fingerprints and blood on it at a murder scene," he said. "Ballistics make it as the weapon used in three shootings at that location."

I sighed. "If Big Brother knows everybody's genetic code, then why do you need me?"

"Because this guy is a pro and he doesn't want to be found." Jordan held up the picture again.

"And you think I've got a line on him somehow and can lead you to him?"

Jordan nodded.

"Loosen your tie," I said. "It's cutting off the flow of oxygen to your brain."

The agent sighed and sat down. "I know your blood type, your service record from start to finish. I know where your mother lives. I know your army buddy Olson is now a gunrunner and that he sold a dozen pallets of Chinese SKSs to a polygamist from Arizona two weeks ago."

I remained silent.

"And I know about Mike Baxter." Jordan smiled, clearly enjoying himself. "I can end his stay at the veterans hospital and put him on the street within the hour. Literally the street, too. No indigent care for him at the local dump-and-run. He'll die at a homeless shelter, screaming in pain because he has no scrips and no money to get them filled even if he did."

"You really drank the Kool-Aid, didn't you?" I tried to control my anger. "You'd do that to a decorated war veteran all in the name of national security?"

"I'm not doing anything to him; you are," he said. "Again."

CHAPTER FORTY-ONE

Ten minutes later I was in the parking lot in front of Ari's, free to go. Jordan gave me a card with his contact info on it, including a cell number. I told him I would help as he'd left me little choice. After he drove off with the uniformed agents, I tore up the card into little bits and let the pieces drift with the wind across the hot asphalt. I figured he could find me if he really wanted to and that Mike Baxter had a few days before getting bounced to the street.

The parking lot was empty. All the customers had left while the FBI man questioned me. Stinky Larry stood beside me, sweating like a redneck at the opera.

"Ari is pissed." Stink shook his head and stared at the ground.

"Tell me something new."

"Says you're banned for life."

"Even Christmas?"

"We're not open on Christmas." Stinky Larry looked up, a perplexed look on his face.

"That's a joke."

"Oh." He chewed on a sweat-speckled lip for a moment. "Ari also says I'm supposed to teach you a lesson."

I sighed and rolled my eyes.

"I don't really want to—"

"On account of you don't want your sweating ass handed to you?"

Larry nodded and mumbled something under his breath.

" 'Bye, Stink." I headed toward the VW.

"Heya, Hank, wait up a sec, willya?" Larry motioned for me to stop. "If it ever comes up, tell Ari I gave it to you good, okay?"

"No problem, Stink." I kept walking.

I drove north on Grand Avenue, past a half-mile stretch of one-story buildings that used to house payday pawnshops, biker bars, and greasy restaurants termed *authentic* because of the surly waitstaff.

Now the elderly brick structures were filled with neighborhood *mercado*s, tiny *taquerias,* and nightclubs with names like Los Dos Hermanos and La Cantina del Corazón, places that had Tejano music on Fridays and rap bands from Laredo on Saturdays.

Maybe half the cars on the street had a Mexican flag decal pasted on a bumper or a window, the rest a statue of the Virgin Mary glued to the dash. The sidewalks were crowded with working men and women and their families, threading past each other, laughing and smiling and generally enjoying life.

After a few blocks of Little Guadalajara, Grand Avenue gave way to the Tenison Park municipal golf course, the street now canopied by towering live oaks and maples. Emerald green swathes of fairway stretched on either side.

A few minutes later I entered the Lakewood section of Dallas, skirting the edges of White Rock Lake, the namesake of the area. I'd lived not far from this part of town, not so many months before, in a snug cottage on a street full of *paisanos* I was proud to call my friends.

Then a very bad man burned my cottage to the ground, very nearly with me in it, retribution for an act I had yet to commit, and I started on the slow, nauseating spiral downward from the vainglorious pinnacle upon which I had set myself.

I drove with no destination in mind as the tidy homes of East Dallas drifted by the windscreen of Anita Nazari's VW. I debated going back to my motel room, ordering a pizza, and watching Oprah. I rubbed the raw spot on my wrists from where the handcuffs and been fastened.

My cell phone rang.

"Yeah-ello." I stopped for the light at Mockingbird Lane and Abrams. There was a place a few hundred yards down Mockingbird called the First and Ten, a dive bar with darkened windows and a flickering flat screen on one wall. Maybe I could get them to switch to Oprah.

"You fucking piece of shit." Nolan's voice teetered on the edge of unhinged.

"Good afternoon to you, too."

"I fucking hate you." New territory for my former partner. The list of people and things she hated was long and ever growing, but yours truly had never been on it before.

"H-h-he kicked me out." Emotion choking her words. Sobbing. Another first. Nolan didn't cry. She shot things, beat up lowlifes, but she didn't cry.

"Who did?" I turned right toward the First and Ten as the light changed. "Rufus?"

"You piece of shit, you . . . you . . ." Her diatribe dissolved into tears.

"Nolan?"

Nothing but sobs.

"Tell me what happened." I pulled into the parking lot of the bar. I could taste the first sip of Shiner Bock, feel it hitting the back of my throat.

"This was my ticket." Her voice was ragged. "I was out of the life. But you screwed it up for me."

"What are you talking about?" A cute redhead in a black Miata parked next to me and got out. She had on a very short denim skirt. She smiled once in my direction before disappearing into the bar.

"Max." She sobbed some more. "Goober fucking Max."

"What about him?" I forgot about the girl in the denim skirt.

"S-s-somebody took him out, this morning."

CHAPTER FORTY-TWO

I headed east on Mockingbird, weaving through traffic, Nolan still on the phone. In the middle of the afternoon, going east or west in the city was tough.

"Talk to me." I punched the accelerator and blew through the yellow-going-red light at Greenville Avenue.

"Some soccer mom found his body behind a Dumpster in Preston Center."

"When?" Preston Center was in the geographical center of the most upscale part of the city, a half-mile square of high-rise offices and apartments and expensive shops clustered around Northwest Highway and Preston Road. Preston Center was a great place to dispose of a body if you didn't care that it would be found.

"This morning sometime." Nolan sounded like she had regained a little composure even though static filled my earpiece. I realized she was on a cell phone and driving. She told me that Max's mother had called Rufus about two hours ago, and Rufus had confronted Nolan immediately thereafter. Rufus said it was her fault, because of her association with me. Told her she had twenty-four hours to get out.

"Where are you now?" I said.

"I just parked in front of the Time Out Tavern."

"Good idea. Getting loaded in the middle of the afternoon will make everything better." I crossed Central Expressway, the north-south dividing line between East Dallas and the rest of the city. "Wait for me. I'm ten minutes away."

Eleven minutes later I parked next to her Cadillac Escalade in front of the black-and-white-striped awning that had been designed to look like a referee's uniform. The awning was a signpost for the Time Out Tavern, a sports bar that had served as my office for a period of time after the landlord at my real one ran me out.

I got out of the VW and hopped into the passenger seat of the Caddy. The windows were so tinted that the interior seemed like midnight.

"He let you keep the car?"

"Shut up, Hank." Her eyes were red-rimmed, swollen.

"Let's go."

"Where?"

"Dork Central." I pointed west on Lovers Lane. Max's place was only a few blocks away. "I need to get into his apartment before the heat does."

"Are you nuts?"

"What's the worst thing that can happen? Rufus kicks you out *more*?"

She turned and stared at me.

"Whatever is going on is way outside the bell curve. Men in black, secret agent stuff." I fastened my seat belt and told her about my activities of the past few days, the assault on the Irish Traveler camp and the encounter with the gung-ho FBI agent. I left out the come-on from Anita Nazari.

"You boinked the doctor lady, didn't you?" Nolan stared at my shirt and then leaned over and looked at my shoes. "Why else would you be dressed like a *GQ* model, huh?"

"I did not sleep with my client. And why have you always been fascinated with my sex life?"

"Fuck a duck, Hank. My stepson gets murdered and you can't even keep your pants zipped." Nolan left a strip of rubber on the cement as she backed out of the parking spot, causing cars on Lovers Lane to screech tires and honk horns.

I didn't say anything, more than a little sure that I had in fact been the cause of the turbo geek's death.

A few minutes later Nolan idled the Escalade down the street where Max had lived with his mother. This section of town was heavily wooded, the streets without curbs or sidewalks, and except for the occasional roar of a jet from Love Field a few thousand yards to the west, casual observers might have been fooled into thinking they'd found a sliver of small-town Norman Rockwell.

Nothing much was going on anywhere except for trucks full of yard equipment and yards full of Hispanic men, much like Anita Nazari's neighborhood, a constant in any residential setting.

We drove past the house on our right. Max's Nissan Xterra was the only car visible, nestled in the garage.

"Somebody boosted him," I said.

"Looks that way." Nolan nodded and stopped at the stop sign at the end of the block, behind a gray Mercury Marquis. The sedan turned right.

I motioned for Nolan to turn left. "Make the block and then go down the alley."

She drove slowly but purposefully, eyes never resting but her head never moving either. Both of us were quiet, back in the zone. I felt a tingle of adrenaline course through my system.

We turned the corner onto the street running perpendicular to Max's. The gray Marquis sat on the side of the street, near the corner, opposite the block we were interested in. The location was where I would have stopped if I was interested in Max's apartment but didn't want to park in front and be obvious.

"What?" Nolan must have sensed my interest.

"The Mercury." I nodded once. "Keep going. Let's do a loop."

We passed the car. The interior was empty.

"You still friendly with that cop?" I wrote down the license plate.

"What cop?"

"The undercover guy that kept asking you out."

"No, Hank, I'm not." Nolan sighed loudly, her tone in that middle ground between mildly miffed and angry. "When you get married, your spouse generally doesn't want some greasy, wrapped-too-tight narc sniffing around."

"Too bad. We could run the plates."

Nolan didn't reply, making loops around the blocks surrounding Max's place. Nothing out of the ordinary. More lawn crews, various repairmen, and occasionally what appeared to be residents.

"Okay, head down the alley," I said.

"Your wish is my command." Nolan turned as requested. The Marquis was still there, but a man in a suit was now bent over the open trunk while a woman with an infant on one hip stood a few feet away. "There. It's a resident. You satisfied now?"

I nodded and wondered how damaged my street radar was after so many months off.

The alley's surface had been covered in concrete at some point, though it now resembled a rock-strewn path, weeds growing in big patches where the pavement had disappeared. The trees lining either side were unkempt, entwined with each other and woven in among the various utility lines.

After a few dozen yards, Nolan stopped the Escalade. "This is it." She pointed to the two-story structure on the left.

I recognized the gray siding, saw the stairs leading to Max's apartment through the tangle of vines and trees that had almost swallowed the chain-link fence.

"I'll be quick." I opened the door. "Wait for my call, ten minutes tops."

"Crap." Nolan held up a pink Motorola. "Almost out of juice."

"You used to charge your phone every night." I got out of the Caddy.

The air in the alley was steamy and smelled sour. Coffee grounds. Spoiled meat. Grease.

"Out of the business, remember?" She dug through the contents of the console. "I've got a charger in here somewhere."

I shut the door and walked around the back of the truck, my new shirt sticky against my torso. The gate opened easily given its age. After a quick check of the garage to make sure no one had pulled in during the thirty seconds since we'd last driven by, I headed to the stairs, taking them two at a time as quietly as possible.

The door was ajar, and I knew instantly I was too late. I stood to one side and pushed it open with a foot.

Nothing.

I stepped into what had been Max's home.

The place had been trashed. The monitors were still intact, but all the computers had been ripped apart, hard drives missing. Books and magazines were scattered everywhere, clothes ripped from their hangers and left lying on the floor. The odor of mint and soap hung over the room; they had hit the bathroom hard, too.

I went into the tiny tiled room and found shaving cream cans that had been punctured and then ripped apart, emptied shampoo bottles, aspirin tablets dotting the floor like oversized snowflakes. I took apart what was left of the small quarters, going as fast as possible, aware that Max's mother might return at any moment from the crime scene or the morgue or wherever it was that women go when their grown children meet a violent end too early in the game.

Nothing of any use. More time to sift might help, but I seriously doubted it. Professionals usually don't leave much behind.

I sat down on Max's mattress, the bed linens a tangled mess on the other side of the room. A rumpled, year-old copy of *Maxim* lay on the floor, the cover featuring a porn star trying to go legit by appearing as the centerfold with her clothes on.

I picked it up and rifled through the pages. Unfortunately, the searchers had mangled it and ripped half of them out. The porn star pics were MIA. Bummer.

Several glossy sheets from another magazine fell out. *Business Week.* A stock analysis of some multinational company with a hard-to-pronounce name mixed in with what looked like sections from a copy of an aviation publication.

I let the mess drop to the floor and stood up. The AC was off, and the room was hot and still, even with the door open.

The sound of the wooden stairs creaking outside seemed as loud as a gunshot.

I froze, remembering the gray Marquis. I reached for the knife in my belt and crept toward the door.

CHAPTER FORTY-THREE

Wood creaked nearby as a leaf blower fired up down the block. The wall adjacent to the stairs shifted slightly, a faint screech the only indication that someone had leaned against the side of the apartment trying to ease his weight as he made his way upstairs.

No question now. The visitor was going for a surreptitious approach, which pretty much ruled out a friendly.

Nowhere to go. Noplace to hide. One way in and out. The doors to both the bathroom and the closet had been removed, and I was in one big room.

And no time left.

Footsteps louder now, no longer trying to be quiet. The rush was on.

I dashed to the door as Rufus ran into the room, a pistol in his hand. He saw me at the same time I lunged. Got my fingers on the top of the gun as he brought it up.

I wrenched the weapon free with my right hand, giving him a shove with my opposite shoulder.

He fell to the ground, rolled over once, and hopped up, standing in front of me in a crouch like an aged cougar ready for one last attack. He wore tennis clothes, white shorts and polo shirt, and sneakers. His face was flushed and dappled with sweat, eyes red-rimmed.

"Not that it matters to you, but I'm sorry for your loss." I pointed the gun, a Beretta nine-millimeter, at the center of his chest. "Just don't take it out on Nolan. It's not her fault."

"Went running to you, did she? That figures." He stood straight up and took several deep breaths. "What are you doing here?"

"Looking for answers, but I don't know the questions to ask."

"So you admit it was your fault." His breathing was ragged. "Y-y-you're the one responsible for my boy's death."

I started to say something but didn't, the right words not available at the moment.

"You're alive. But my son is dead."

"The fat lady hasn't sung yet."

"You'll live. I know your type." Rufus took a deep breath and stood up straight. "You're a cockroach; you'll survive anything . . . almost."

"Don't do the threat thing, okay?" I lowered the pistol. "It's very unbecoming on you."

"I keep good records, track things on a day-to-day basis." He wiped his brow with a handkerchief. "Yesterday my portfolio was worth sixty-five million and change."

"Good for you." I wondered if Nolan had signed a prenup. I didn't ask.

"From this day forward, every dime of it will be devoted to crushing you." He stuck the handkerchief back in his pocket. "You'll wish you were dead, but I'll make sure that doesn't happen for a good long while."

"Anger poisons a man's soul." I dropped the clip from the bottom of the pistol before yanking back the slide and ejecting a round from the chamber.

"A philosopher you're not." He turned and surveyed the wreckage of his son's room. "Who did this?"

"If I knew I wouldn't be here."

He turned back around and stared at me for a long time. "A kneecap, I'm thinking."

"Huh?"

"You won't know when, but sometime in the next few months somebody is gonna blow away one of your kneecaps." He smiled. "That's just a start. Now get the fuck out of here and let me grieve."

I dropped the pistol on the mattress but stuck the clip and the extra bullet in my pocket before heading down the stairs. Once in the overgrown backyard, I dialed Nolan's cell. The call went straight to voice mail.

I threaded my way through the vegetation to the back of the garage, where I figured she'd be waiting.

The Escalade was idling two lots down in a wide space on the side of the alley. Nolan flashed the lights once and headed my way.

The Caddy slowed. I jumped into the passenger seat and said, "Let's get the hell out of here."

She gunned it, going too fast down the narrow lane.

"Try not to kill us, willya?" I blew out a lungful of air and noticed her hair was messed up, tangled and in her face. "Hey, you okay?"

She didn't answer. Instead the mop of hair turned, and I saw my face reflected in a pair of mirrored sunglasses.

CHAPTER FORTY-FOUR

I went for the door and my blade at the same time. The door had auto locks. The knife got tangled in my belt and love handles.

The man in the wig gave me an elbow to the temple. I saw it coming, tried to avoid the blow. Failed. The other side of my skull connected with the tinted window. The last thing on my mind as the lights went out was why pages from a *BusinessWeek* article on a multinational cor- poration would be jammed inside a tattered copy of *Maxim*.

Minutes, days, or years later, my head began to throb, cheap-tequila bad. I opened my eyes.

The man from Federal Agent John Jordan's photo stood in front of me. The wig was gone. He wore a pair of tinted glasses. The sunlight streaming through the live oak trees overhead sparkled on the lenses.

I was lying on my side on a thick bed of St. Augustine grass. A house was visible behind the man, a temporary chain-link fence encircling it, windows gone, gaps where an AC unit would go. A teardown, waiting for the wrecking ball.

I tried to move. Hands bound behind my back with something sticky, duct tape maybe. Head hurt more. A plane screamed overhead, and I realized we were still near Love Field. I had only been out for a few minutes.

"You're getting involved in something you shouldn't," the man said. "I would have hoped our first meeting in Weatherford would have made that clear."

I closed my eyes and willed the pain away from my skull. "W-w-where's Nolan?"

"Your friend is in the car."

"What did you do to her?" I opened my eyes.

"A mild tranquilizer. Should wear off in an hour or so." He coughed and clutched his chest.

"I didn't catch your name." I tensed my wrists against the duct tape, felt very little movement.

"Names are meaningless in an age of numbers." His coughing lessened, and he smiled. "Let's just say I'm a professional, the one they call when they need something off the books."

"Word I hear is that you're a rogue."

The smile slid off his face. "Who told you that?"

I didn't say anything.

He walked over to where I lay and knelt beside me. A faint stench of chemicals emanated from his body, not unlike the aura surrounding Mike Baxter in the hospital room.

"I was a Ranger, too. Served in the Gulf War, and later." His face was impassive, hard to read behind the glasses. "We have a bond. Don't make me do things to you we will both regret."

I didn't reply.

"I spent seven weeks in an Iraqi prison in 1998." He smiled tightly. "Would you like me to show you some stuff I learned there?"

"The FBI," I said. "They had a picture of you. Said you'd switched teams."

"But of course. That makes perfect sense." He sat down on the grass, cross-legged. His breathing was ragged, congestion rattling in his throat and lungs. "Problems. Opportunities. Pleasure and pain. Where does the line between them lie?"

"Huh?"

"The enemy is in the mirror more often than not." His face was drawn and gray except for a spiderweb of burst capillaries in his cheeks, the complexion of a hard drinker but without the booze-induced puffiness.

"If you say so." I twisted one wrist and felt the tape loosen a tiny bit.

"I mean no harm. You must know this." He leaned forward.

"Riddle me this, Batman." I rolled over and managed to get to my knees. "Are you the one after Anita Nazari or is there another player around?"

He smiled for a moment before removing the glasses. One eye was solid red save for the dark dot of a pupil in the center.

I gasped. The contractor, Collin Toogoode, must have seen him without the shades. And now both brothers were dead.

"Are you a student of history?" The man stood up. He was wobbly on his feet.

"I bought the *Playboy* fiftieth anniversary book. Does that count?" I tried for humor as my skin went cold at the implications of his most recent action, the removal of the glasses.

"Do you realize the amount of poison Americans place on their lawns every year, the tons of pesticides that drip into the groundwater?" He stroked the dried and dying bed of St. Augustine grass.

I wondered for a moment if I had stumbled on some new brand of ecoterrorist. But Anita Nazari wasn't strip mining or selling SUVs. She was a doctor, fooling around with test tubes.

"Eisenhower was right." He replaced the glasses on his face before pulling a brown bottle of what looked like vitamins or supplements from a canvas back on the ground. The label was familiar, but I couldn't place it.

"Dwight was before my time," I said.

"Beware the military-industrial complex." He shook a couple of capsules into his mouth before taking a long drink from a glass bottle of mineral water.

"Fortunary." I said the name of the multinational corporation that I had read on the pages hidden in the men's magazine.

The man in the mirrored sunglasses paused in midswallow.

"That company is a part of this, isn't it?"

"Resourceful. Observant. Diligent." The man nodded. "Everything they said about you is true. Unfortunately your very tenacity is going to be your death sentence."

"Let's not get carried away, okay, Mr. Secret Agent Man?" I felt my flesh get colder even as sweat dribbled down my skin.

"You know that name." He pulled a knife from his pocket. "And you must die because of it."

My head pounded. I swiveled, looking for a way out of the backyard.

"Oh, that's too rich." The man laughed. "*I'm* not going to kill you. If the game still had teams, we'd be on the same side."

"But the glasses?" I blinked sweat out of my eyes. "Y-you took them off."

He held the knife in front of me. It was the Spyderco that had been in my waistband.

"It's the end of the fourth quarter. Your time on the field is over." He tossed the blade into the bushes behind me and walked toward the front yard.

CHAPTER FORTY-FIVE

It took me twenty minutes to find the knife and cut the duct tape away. I peeled the last bit off my wrists and stuck the Spyderco back in my belt.

I was drenched, the humid air in the backyard of the soon-to-be-demolished house cloying with the scent of moldy wood and long-unkempt honeysuckle vines.

I found a garden hose underneath an overgrown holly bush. I turned on the faucet, but nothing came out.

The Escalade was parked in the garage of the house, the windows down. The structure was hidden from the street by a row of cedar trees.

Nolan was in the back, unconscious, clothes soaked in sweat.

I grabbed a half-liter bottle of spring water from the floorboard of the backseat. The liquid was tepid but welcome. I drank several big gulps before splashing some on her face.

Her eyes fluttered open. "W-w-where am I?"

"It's okay." I held the bottle to her lips. "Drink a little."

She took a sip and gagged. I held her upright. Patted her on the back. Gave her another few ounces. She swallowed this time.

"W-w-wha—" Her body went slack, eyes rolling back in her head, breathing deep and regular. I carried her to the front passenger seat. The keys were in the ignition. I started the Caddy and cranked the AC on high, closing the windows as I backed out of the gravel driveway.

I didn't recognize the street, lined on either side by towering oaks and magnolias. The road itself was bumpy, more like a country lane than a suburban avenue. Most of the houses were barely visible, half hidden behind brick walls and wrought-iron fencing laced with shrubbery.

After a half mile or so I stopped when the narrow street T-boned into Northwest Highway, a major road bisecting this part of the city.

I took my bearings. To the west or left was Love Field. To the east was Preston Center, where Max's body had been found. And Nolan's house.

For a moment I thought about getting the VW but figured I would be better off in a car that the FBI didn't know about yet.

I headed toward the home Nolan and Rufus shared. I called Anita Nazari's cell, got no answer. Left a terse message for her to call me back.

The quickest way to Nolan's was to take the Dallas Tollway south to Lovers Lane and head east from there.

I was stopped at the light at Northwest Highway and the Tollway when I saw the first helicopter. It was black or dark gray and completely devoid of markings. It came from the south and stopped over the intersection, hovering. In the distance I could see another one, circling a few hundred feet above the cluster of office towers at Preston Center.

The Escalade sat higher than most of the other cars, giving me an excellent view of the surrounding traffic. Two navy blue Crown Victorias, each with a forest of antennas on top, were idling next to each other at the stoplight on the opposite side of the Tollway, facing the Escalade.

Nolan stirred in the seat beside me. She opened her eyes for a moment. "Ch-ch-choppers?"

The light changed. I followed a half-dozen other vehicles onto the southbound lanes of the Tollway.

The helicopter rotated its nose southward and skittered in the same direction.

"What the hell . . ." I kept my hands tight on the wheel, trying to figure out how they knew.

"N-n-no police, 'kay?" Nolan opened her eyes for a moment before snoring again.

I skipped the Lovers Lane exit and drove on to the next one south, Mockingbird. The helicopter followed, dangling lazily over the highway.

Three other cars that had got on at Northwest Highway exited with me.

"The cell phone." I stopped at the light. That explained the second chopper over the office towers at Preston Center. All of the buildings had rooftop cell stations.

As if on cue, the second black copter appeared on the southern horizon as if it were backing up its mate. No sign of the two government Fords.

The vehicle next to me was a late model Chevy Silverado. When the light changed, I rolled down the window and tossed my phone into the pickup's bed.

I turned left.

The Chevy turned left, too.

"Crap." I turned left again at the next street.

The Chevy followed suit, as did the helicopters.

We all rode in a weird multidimensional convoy until I abruptly turned right down a narrow residential street. The Chevy kept going. I exhaled loudly and rolled to a stop at the end of the block.

"Where are we?" Nolan sat up, blinking.

I told her quickly what had happened. She remembered nothing of the attack by the operative who had impersonated her in order to trick me.

"Where are you going now?" She rubbed her eyes.

"Your house."

She sighed melodramatically. "I have no home."

"The guy loaded you up with God knows what." I turned onto University Boulevard, which dead-ends in the Southern Methodist University Campus, and headed toward Casa Rufus. "You need to rest, get it out of your system."

A few minutes later, I turned onto Rufus's street. An ambulance and two University Park police department squad cars were parked in front of the house, lights flashing.

I sped up.

"Stop." Nolan banged the dash.

I kept going.

"Goddamn you, Hank Oswald." She gave me an elbow in the ribs. "*Stop.*" Her eyes filled with tears.

I stopped a hundred yards past her house.

We both got out and walked to the front door. When we got to the porch, the glass entrance swung open and the backside of an EMT emerged, holding one end of a gurney.

Nolan grabbed my hand.

The rest of the gurney emerged, a body obviously underneath, covered from head to toe. A police officer came outside and approached us.

"Mrs. McAlister?" He called Nolan by her married name.

"Yes." My former partner's voice was strong, but her skin was pasty white.

"I'm sorry." The officer pointed to the gurney. "Your husband had a heart attack." He raised one eyebrow a fraction of an inch as he looked at Nolan's hand clasped in mine. "It was pretty sudden. He didn't suffer."

More police officers emerged. More EMTs. Paperwork.

We sat in the study as various people offered official words of condolence. I kept waiting for someone to ask my name, but no one did. If this had been in another part of town and a man of less wealth and social standing had died, there would have been more inquiries as to my relation to the deceased.

After about half an hour, the Hispanic woman who had let me in the other night arrived. She looked at me and at Nolan, swore once, and left.

Another thirty minutes passed, and we were alone.

"Now what?" I said.

Nolan shrugged but didn't say anything.

"Rufus have any other family you need to call?"

"One dead brother." She stood up. "A couple of nieces. And Max."

"Max is dead, too."

"Yep." Her lip quivered. Eyes filled with tears again.

"Nolan, I'm so sorry." I put my arms around her.

"I-I really loved him." She sobbed on my shoulder.

"I know."

"I shouldn't have said those things about him."

"Shhh." I smoothed her hair as she cried. After a few minutes she pushed herself away and wandered into the kitchen. Pots and pans clanged together. I waited another couple of minutes and then padded after her into the garishly decorated open area overlooking a wood-paneled library that had a green felt pool table in the middle. Several pots were on the Viking range.

"You want something to eat?" she said.

"Sure. Need some help?" I was eager to assist in her domestic efforts since they appeared to be soothing.

"I'm making gumbo."

"From scratch?" I looked at my watch.

Her eyes filled with tears again. She sat down on the floor and hugged her knees to her chest.

I looked at the pots. They were filled with water, nothing else. I turned the gas off and sat down next to my former partner. After a few moments she got up without speaking, walked to the freezer, and pulled out two chicken pot pies.

I stood, too, as she put them in the microwave. Four minutes later we ate. When we were finished she said, "I want to fuck somebody up."

"Me, too." I took a long drink of ice water.

"But who?"

"Don't know." I put the glass in the sink. "But I bet Anita Nazari does."

CHAPTER FORTY-SIX

I didn't go to Nazari's house. I wheeled the Cadillac into the parking lot in front of an organic chain grocery store, a few doors down from the bookstore where I had stopped before meeting Anita a few days before.

"Why are we going shopping?" Nolan said. The center was busy, people moving about, wheeling carts full of groceries to their cars.

"This guy is sick." I parked the black Escalade next to a white Escalade.

"Gee, Hank. You figured that out all on your own?" Nolan shook her head. "*All* the bad guys are messed up. And so are most of the good ones."

"That's not what I meant." I opened the door. "He's sick physically; something's wrong with him."

Nolan got out and followed me into the store, past the throngs of suburban moms buying overpriced produce and laundry detergent safe for tree huggers of all persuasions.

Originally patterned after a typical health food store, the place had long since morphed into a mega-holistic shopping experience, designed more or less like a regular large grocery store but with an emphasis on organic foodstuffs and environmentally safe products. The decor was earth tones, brown walls, polished hardwood and tile floorings, subdued lighting. One side was loaded with appealing displays of produce. The meat counter was in the back, aisles of nonperishable items in the center.

I headed toward the middle, where I knew the vitamins were displayed. Nolan followed a few steps behind me. The air smelled different from a typical food store, the scent of fruit and produce heavier, not tanged by the harsh chemicals found in the bug sprays and other items on the hardware aisle of a regular grocery.

"Where are we going?" Nolan said.

I ignored her and stopped in front of a guy unpacking a carton marked VITAMIN C, 1,000 MILLIGRAMS. He was in his late thirties, hair in dreadlocks, with rings in his nose, ears, and lips.

"I'm looking for someone," I said.

"This isn't that kind of store." He stuck a bottle on a shelf.

"A guy about fifty. Medium height and weight. Average looking."

"A good-looking Republican like you?" He smirked. "Figured your type would go for something younger."

Nolan swallowed a laugh.

"The guy wears glasses all the time."

Dreadlocks paused with a bottle in midair. He looked up at me.

"You know who I'm talking about, don't you?"

"Why are you looking for him?" He put the bottle back in the carton and stood up.

"He's sick."

"I'll say. Immune system fried like that." Dreadlocks looked over my shoulder, where I knew Nolan was standing. "Who are you two?"

"I'm trying to help." I smiled. "Do you know what happened to him?"

"Toxins, dude." The man waved his hand at nothing. "A hazard of modern-day living. Poisons we produce are everywhere. People get an overload and are never the same."

"Like from an oil field fire?" I said, more to myself than to him. "Petroleum."

"Right on. Half my customers suffer from environmental illness." Dreadlocks's voice took on a preachy, self-righteous tone. "The capitalist model is only interested in profits, not the damage their greed does to the world . . . and to us."

"Save the politics for the next Greenpeace rally." Nolan rolled her eyes. "And what the hell is environmental illness?"

"People get exposed to too many toxins, they get sick." He shrugged, trying for holier-than-thou. "All different kinds of ways. Immune disorders. Cancer. Hell, what do you think chronic fatigue syndrome is?"

I thought about Mike Baxter. "When did you last see this guy?"

"You never told me who you are." Dreadlocks crossed his arms.

"Hey, sicko." Nolan grabbed one of the guy's rings and twisted. "When's the last time you saw the sicko?"

"*Owww.*" The man reached for her hand, but Nolan twisted harder. "T-t-tonight. B-b-buying antioxidants . . . just a few min—"

It began to snow.

Little white capsules showered down all over us a nanosecond after the distinctive metal clang of a silenced firearm echoed down the narrow aisle. Nolan let go of Dreadlocks, shoving him into the vitamin E section. Bottles crashed to the tile floor.

I caught a glimpse of a man in khakis and a golf sweater at the end of the row farthest from the front. The man from this afternoon, the operative from the FBI agent's photograph. He was wearing those weird, lightly tinted glasses and carrying what looked like a Ruger .22 with an extra-thick barrel, indicating a built-in suppresser.

Dreadlocks stood and shook his head a couple of times, greasy, matted hair flying everywhere.

The man in the glasses fired again. He hit his target this time.

Dreadlocks swatted at the back of his head as if he'd been bitten by a mosquito. He stood still for a moment before his eyes rolled back and he dropped onto the pile of broken vitamin bottles.

Nolan dived behind a display case of fiber pills.

I stood still and stared at the man in the glasses, plainly aware of my exposure, but also knowing on some level that he meant me no harm.

He nodded once and darted away.

"Let's go." I tapped Nolan on the shoulder and headed toward the front of the store. She followed, but the floor was oily with burst vitamin tablets, and we both slipped. I landed on the carton of vitamin C that Dreadlocks had been unloading, Nolan on top of me.

"Is that him?" She hopped off. "The guy from this afternoon?"

"Yeah." I rolled off the carton and moved as fast as possible on the slick floor toward the front.

The store was even more crowded now, all of the cashier lanes open and stacked up with people. Children everywhere, running in the aisles, playing.

The man in the glasses was about thirty yards away, by a display case of gourmet cheeses. He looked at me and shook his head slowly.

I pressed through the crowd, kids coursing on either side of me. He was headed toward the door. I was closer, but he had less traffic in his way.

A tall, gangly boy about eleven with fingers flying across a Game Boy yelled as I eased him away. "Hey!" He jumped back and knocked over a stack of organic canned beans.

"What the hell do you think you're doing?" A man I took to be his father grabbed my arm. He had the insolent look of an overbearing dad who bullied the coaches at football games.

"Sorry." I tried to pull away. "My little girl is lost, over by the cheese."

"You hurt my son." Righteous indignation now.

The boy read the situation and began to cry, not a very believable performance on someone who was nearing six feet tall and had the beginnings of a mustache.

The shooter in the glasses sidestepped an overweight woman with a basket full of food and headed toward the door. He smiled once as he saw my predicament.

"Excuse me." A manager type appeared from between two tanned and anorexic soccer moms. "Is there a problem here?" He looked at the crying boy and then at me.

"This guy shoved my son." The dad pointed my way. "Where's security? He could be one of those sexual predators I read about."

"Hold on, now. Everything is cool," Nolan said. "My friend accidentally tripped."

"Who are you?" The manager grabbed my other arm.

Somebody screamed from the vitamin aisle.

"No time to chitchat." Nolan kicked the manager in the knee, followed by an elbow to the solar plexus. He fell on top of the beans. The father let go of my arm and looked at Nolan.

"You did tell Junior that he was second choice at the orphanage, right?" Nolan shoved the kid into his dad and headed toward the door.

The crowd was more erratic now, aware that something was going on, people talking louder than normal, moving and craning their necks to see whatever was happening.

The man in the glasses slipped through the door and into the dusk as I tumbled over a basket full of produce.

Nolan pulled me up. Together we threaded our way through the crowd of shoppers who were on the edge of mass hysteria. The words "dead body" swept across the room, following us to the door.

Once outside, I ran to the curb and looked for the shooter.

"You really think you're gonna find him?" Nolan came up beside me and pointed to the parking lot, now jammed with even more cars and shoppers. Horns honked. People pointed to the organic grocery store, talking with each other. Every fourth person seemed to be on a cell phone. At the far end of the shopping center, blue and red lights strobed as a Plano police cruiser tried to get through the crowds.

"We need to boogie." Nolan grabbed my arm and pulled me toward the Escalade.

I followed her, got in. Cranked the ignition.

"He took out the guy with dreadlocks but not us," Nolan said.

"I know." I backed out and headed away from the store, the crowds of people slow to move out of my way.

"Why?"

"He doesn't want us to know that he's sick."

"What the hell does that mean?"

I didn't answer. I turned the Cadillac north and headed toward Anita Nazari's house.

CHAPTER FORTY-SEVEN

We passed several more shopping centers, each lit up like an airport runway and looking like the one before, a monotonous strip of faux charm with the same chain stores dominating, the order of their lineup the only distinction.

I turned onto the street leading into her subdivision, past a set of large stone columns delineating this particular neighborhood. The edifices were designed to look like the walls of a castle, a subtle reminder to those who did not belong that they weren't welcome. I wondered if the tower of stones provided a sense of security to the residents.

Nolan appeared impatient, drumming her nails on the top of the console.

"We need a gun," she said.

"No time." I turned onto Anita's street and drove past the house under construction.

"Nice casa." Nolan unbuckled her seat belt as the Escalade stopped in front of Anita's house. "You could do worse, you know. A doctor, making good coin."

"I'm pretty sure she's crazy." I shut the door and headed up the sidewalk.

"That's never been an issue before." Nolan walked across the grass and peered into the living room window. "Remember that TV reporter, the one who made Christmas stockings after your first date for the kids you two were gonna have together?"

I ignored her and rang the bell, standing to one side of the door, the old habits returning easily.

No answer.

Nolan joined me on the porch, on the opposite side, her old habits kicking in as well.

I rang again and waited another thirty seconds before pressing the door with the heel of my hand. It opened easily, an alarm chime sounding from the interior. I stepped inside. Nolan followed, leaving the door ajar.

A light was on in the kitchen. Otherwise the house was dark.

I eased down the hallway, past the stairs.

Anita was sitting at the counter, staring at the laptop. She looked up when I entered.

"Why didn't you get the door?" I said.

"I thought it was Tom," she said. "I tried your cell, but no one answered."

"They were tracking me." I looked around the kitchen and family room. Mira was nowhere to be seen. "I had to throw it away. Where's your daughter?"

"Upstairs, asleep." A long pause. "And who is your little friend?" Anita nodded toward Nolan, her tone saccharine.

"I'm Hank's associate." Nolan moved toward the back door, flanking out. "We're not bumping uglies, if that's what you're worried about."

Anita frowned. "I beg your pardon?"

"You need to get out of here," I said.

"No." Anita stood up. "I'm tired of running."

"Then why do you have luggage by the door?" Nolan pointed to two suitcases.

"An observant one, this associate of yours."

"Don't avoid the question," I said.

"We used to live in a beautiful home in the Niavaran district of Tehran." Anita spoke to me as she opened the refrigerator and pulled out a bottle of white wine. "It was whitewashed limestone, with bougainvillea and roses in the garden."

Nolan stood by the back door and shot me a look, one eyebrow raised.

"Maybe we could talk about this some other time," I said.

"My father was a doctor, too. We had many servants."

"This is a government operation of some sort," I said. "You need to get out of here as soon as possible."

"He died when I was eighteen." Anita poured a glass of wine. "After Tehran, he lived in a third-floor walk-up flat in Stuttgart, behind a cement plant. Worked as a nurse."

"I'm sorry about the traumatic childhood and all." I walked around the counter until we were only a few feet away. "But you need to listen to what I'm saying."

"Mira and I are going to Los Angeles tomorrow." She drank half the glass in one swallow. "I have an interview at UCLA the next day."

"Then that leaves tonight." I looked at her laptop. The browser was open to the main page for American Airlines.

"Come with us, Hank." She smiled. "We could start a new life together."

"No, this is where I live." I wanted to say more but couldn't find the right words. How many of us don't dream of starting over, getting a life mulligan?

"You'll take care of me for tonight, then, won't you, Hank?" Her voice turned seductive. "And maybe tomorrow we can leave on an adventure?"

I didn't hear the door open. I didn't sense the intrusion. Nolan hissed.

I didn't know what was about to happen until the muzzle of the government-issued Sig Sauer was a few feet from my temple.

Special Agent John Jordan held the pistol in the Bureau-sanctioned two-handed grip. "Hands on top of your head. Now."

CHAPTER FORTY-EIGHT

I did as instructed, fingers laced together, palms on the top of my scalp.

"You, too." Jordan looked at Nolan.

She didn't move.

"I'm the FBI, honey." He waved the gun at her. "This ain't like tracking down deadbeat husbands. I will smoke you where you stand if you don't comply."

Nolan slowly put her hands on top of her head.

A second agent in an ill-fitting gray suit entered the room, handcuffs in his hand.

"What is the meaning of this?" Anita gave Jordan her best self-righteous physician tone.

"Dr. Nazari, right?" Jordan holstered his weapon before pulling my hands behind my back and slapping a pair of cuffs on my wrists. They probably were the same pair used earlier in the day. The second agent did the same to Nolan.

"That is my name," Anita said. "And this is my home. Why are you here?"

"You are being threatened, correct?" Jordan spun me around and walked me to where Nolan was sitting, back against the kitchen wall, legs spread.

"Yes, but this man is not the one threatening me." Anita pointed at me.

"Right." Jordan blew air out of his mouth in a long sigh. "We *know* that already."

"Then what's with the cuffs?" I let the second agent seat me next to Nolan, hands smashed between my back and the wall.

"You violated our agreement." Jordan knelt beside me so our eyes were level with each other. "Nice little trick, throwing your cell phone into the pickup truck. Now you have officially interfered in a federal investigation. Which is a big no-no."

"What about me?" Nolan said.

"I'm sure we can find something to charge you with." Jordan stood up and pulled a cell phone from his coat pocket. "Like aggravated bad judgment for being a new widow and running off with Oswald. I dunno, we'll figure something out."

"Your guy from the photo is nearby," I said quietly.

"Where?" Jordan quit dialing the cell and looked at me.

"What are you talking about?" Anita slammed her wineglass down on the granite counter.

"We saw him at a store, about a mile from here." I related the rest of the story. "He took out a clerk. There's got to be a lot of radio chatter."

Jordan nodded to the second agent. "Go see, willya? And call it in. We need reinforcements."

The agent left the kitchen, heading toward the front door.

Jordan turned to Anita. "This is about your work, isn't it?"

"I wouldn't know."

"It has to be." The FBI agent nodded slowly. "Nothing else makes sense."

"My research is singularly unspectacular." She crossed her arms. "Chemicals in the blood. I wouldn't expect you to understand."

"Have you recently finished a project?" Jordan put the cell phone back in his pocket.

"Yes." Anita frowned. "It's preliminary, of course, awaiting my signature next week. Why on earth are you asking?"

"It's my job." Jordan smiled and pulled his weapon out. He pointed it at Anita Nazari's head. "Unfortunately, I can't allow you to issue the final report."

"Oh, shit," Nolan said.

I tensed against the cuffs. Metal bit into my wrists.

"What?" Anita blinked repeatedly, face going pale. "You . . . the gun . . . what are you talking about?"

"Your research messed up a lot of things," he said. "And I'm the fix-it person who—"

Clank. The sound was identical to what I had heard in the grocery store.

Jordan lowered his gun. Swayed a little. Turned and looked at me. A thin trail of blood dribbled from his ear. He opened his mouth, but nothing came out.

As he fell over, the man in the golf shirt and mirrored glasses entered Anita Nazari's kitchen. He held the Ruger in his hand and swept the room with its muzzle.

"I should have known." Anita shook her head slowly, her face devoid of any emotion.

The man in the glasses pointed the pistol at me.

"Known what?" I willed my voice to remain calm.

"Hank, please let me introduce you to my husband."

CHAPTER FORTY-NINE

Nobody said anything. The air in the kitchen was cool, but sweat beaded my brow and trickled down the small of my back. Anita Nazari took a long drink of wine and stared at the screen of her laptop.

Nolan spoke first. "I am *so* confused."

"What's your name?" I said to the man.

"It doesn't matter." His voice was deadpan. The muzzle of the gun never wavered from my face. "The name on my birth certificate died on the battlefield."

"Mr. Nazari?" Nolan said.

"I think I'll shoot you first." The man's tone was the same, but the way his shoulders hunched forward betrayed a certain amount of anger I knew I couldn't begin to fathom.

"During an oil field fire, right?" I nodded slowly.

"His name is Captain Josh Pendergast, United States Army." Anita crossed her arms. "Missing, presumed dead during a classified mission somewhere in the Middle East in 1999."

"Are you gonna shoot me, Captain Josh Pendergast?" I nodded at the gun.

He didn't say anything.

"Who do you work for?" I said.

He put a round into the wall between my head and Nolan's.

She flinched. "No more questions for the crazy dude, okay, Hank?"

"Ooo-kay." My voice cracked.

"Why would they not tell me you were alive?" Anita said. "Why would *you* not tell me?"

"It was better that way, don't you think?" Pendergast took several deep breaths. His color was bad, pasty, almost the hue of a corpse. "Avoid what surely would have been a messy divorce."

"What's wrong with you?" Anita must have noticed it, too. "Are you ill?"

Pendergast turned the pistol toward his wife.

"Enough with the melodramatics. Put the gun down, Josh." Anita smirked, her tone light and cheery but in a condescending and belittling way. "You always were a weak man."

"Do you have any idea what an insufferable bitch you are?" He gripped the pistol tighter, knuckles going white.

"Oh, come now." Anita smiled. "You're like all men. You need someone to tell you what to do, where to do it."

"Heya, doctor lady," Nolan said. "Let's not get the whack-job more aggro, okay?"

"I want to kill you now." Pendergast put his free hand on the back of a bar stool and leaned on it for support.

"You don't have the balls to murder the mother of your child," Anita said.

"How is Mira?" He smiled for a moment.

"She has asthma." Anita smirked. "But no father."

"I've dreamed of this moment." His knuckles were white against the grip.

"Then do it. Shoot me." She tapped her chest with one finger. "Go ahead."

"No." He stuck the pistol in his belt. "I won't go against my orders."

"Huh?" I looked at Anita and then at Pendergast.

"Your research is important." Pendergast knelt beside Jordan's corpse and patted his pockets, removing a key ring. "The truth must come out."

"Oh, Josh." Anita's shoulders slumped, her eyes cast downward.

"The truth about what?" I said.

"*Look at me.*" Pendergast stood, the keys jangling at his side. "Look at what has happened to me."

His coloring had changed, face now mottled the color of old maraschino cherries, slick with sweat. His breath rattled in his chest like marbles in a can.

"If the world finds out about the chemicals, it won't fix you," she said. Her tone almost sounded like she cared.

"Nothing can help me." He leaned against the counter. "But there are others . . ." He dropped the keys and slid to the floor.

"Pendergast?" I leaned forward. "You okay?"

"Josh?" Anita came around the counter. She knelt by her husband, placed a finger on his carotid artery.

"The keys." I nodded my head toward where they lay.

"What?" Anita appeared confused.

"Unlock the cuffs."

She grabbed the key ring and rifled through them, stopping at the smallest one. "Is this it?"

"Never know until you try." I stood up awkwardly and turned my back to her.

She fumbled with the ring, but after a few tries she got the key in place and unlocked the cuffs. I freed Nolan as Pendergast shook his head several times and pushed himself to his feet.

"What happened?" he said.

"You checked out for a second." I stuck the cuffs in my pocket along with Jordan's keys.

The four of us turned at the sound of the front doorbell ringing.

"Wonder if that's the pizza I ordered," Nolan said.

Pendergast pulled the Ruger from his belt, but the movement caused him to lose his balance and he almost fell over, steadying himself on the counter.

The front door creaked open and then slammed shut. Lumbering footfalls marched toward the kitchen.

Tom Maguire, Anita's on-again, off-again boyfriend, walked in. He looked at Pendergast and at me and gulped. "W-w-what the heck is going on here?"

"Who are you?" Nolan put her hands on her hips, an incredulous look on her face. "And would someone lock the fucking door?"

"Oh, for God's sake." Anita rolled her eyes. "Tom, why are you here?"

"This is Tom." I sighed and relaxed. "Anita's boyfriend."

Tom frowned and looked at Pendergast, now slumped on a bar stool.

"Let me see if I got this straight." Nolan pushed herself away from the counter and turned to Anita. "By my count, you've slept with a hundred percent of the men in the room right now. Rock on, sister."

"We did *not* have sex," I said. "How many times do I have to tell you?"

"Anita, what are they talking about?" Tom's brow furrowed, trying to figure it all out. "Ohmigod! What the heck is that?" He bounced from one foot to the other, pointing to the corpse of the man who called himself John Jordan.

"That, Tom, is a dead body." I rubbed my eyes, suddenly tired beyond words.

"Oh, jeez." His faced blanched, eyes wide as golf balls. "We gotta call the police." He pulled a cell phone out.

"*No.*" Anita, Nolan, and I spoke at the same time.

Tom froze, the phone in one hand, staring at Anita.

"I know this is difficult for one who has spent his life in the safety of the corporate world, peddling pharmaceuticals to indifferent physicians such as myself." Anita's tone was icy. "But there are times when the police aren't welcome."

Josh Pendergast sat up on the bar stool. Blinked. Looked at Tom.

A chill ran down my spine, and I didn't know why.

"Where's Mira?" Tom's voice was quieter now.

"Upstairs." Anita looked at her ex-husband when she spoke.

"You're a drug rep?" Information clicked in my head, but it still made no sense. "Who do you work for?"

Tom smiled once and squared his shoulders, the bumbling jock persona melting away like a dab of ice cream on hot asphalt.

"Fortunary, right?" I measured the distance from where I stood to the Ruger tucked in the back of Josh Pendergast's belt.

Tom didn't reply. Instead he pulled a Glock from behind his hip and pointed it at Anita Nazari.

CHAPTER FIFTY

I tensed and reached for the gun on my hip that I no longer carried. Nolan took a deep, loud breath. Anita was as still as a stop sign, a look of utter and total incredulity on her face.

"Mama?" Mira's voice sounded sleepy.

Everyone in the room turned to the back stairs, where Anita's daughter stood in a bathrobe. After that, everything happened at once.

Josh Pendergast pushed himself off the bar stool, his head connecting with Tom Maguire's stomach. Nolan grabbed Anita and pushed her toward the door. I lunged for the stairs and Mira.

Sounds of scuffling from the counter. A shot rang out.

I scooped up Mira. Kicked open the back door. Dashed into the yard, running past the pool. I was vaguely aware of footsteps behind me, hoping they belonged to Nolan.

The back gate wouldn't open, despite my repeated latching and un-latching of the locking mechanism.

"Crap." I kicked it.

Nothing.

I hit it with my free hand. Again, nothing.

Another shot sounded from the interior of the house.

Anita pushed me to one side and reached to the top of the wooden gate. The barrier swung open, and the three adults and one child soon found ourselves in the alley behind Anita's suburban house.

"Now what?" Nolan said.

The sound of breaking glass came from the house.

"We get in the Escalade and get the hell out of here." I headed toward the end of the alley, still carrying Mira, Nolan following.

"Wait." Anita hadn't moved. "What about Josh?"

"Doctor lady." Nolan turned around and marched back to where Anita stood. "You have officially crossed the line from being merely annoying to constituting a danger to the rest of us, including your child."

"He's hurt," Anita said.

Nolan grabbed her arm and pulled. "Let's go."

A few moments later, we rounded the corner onto the side street running perpendicular to Anita's block.

"Hang back for a moment." I put Mira on the ground and pointed to a line of shrubs by the alley entrance.

Anita grabbed her child and pressed the youngster's body to her own.

"We really should have stopped for guns," Nolan said.

I crept across the lawn and pressed myself to the side of the house. The Escalade was where we'd left it, parked behind Anita's Range Rover. No one was visible.

I touched the keys in my pocket and eased myself away from the house, preparing to dash for the Cadillac. I froze when the front door of the house opened and a swath of light painted a section of the front lawn.

Tom Maguire's bulky frame staggered out, plodding down the sidewalk. His gait was wobbly, one sleeve of his suit coat torn away, revealing a shoulder covered in a white dress shirt. He held a pistol in each hand, the one in his right appearing to be the Ruger carried by Pendergast.

He walked to the cars parked by the curb. When he got to the Cadillac he fired two silenced shots into the radiator, then repeated the action on the Range Rover. Then he turned toward the corner of the house where I was hiding and staggered toward me.

I slipped away and ran back to where I'd left Nolan with Anita and her child, about thirty yards away.

"We got problems." I kept my voice low.

No answer.

"Nolan?" I squinted in the darkness, the streetlight on the far corner doing little to pierce the night.

Groan.

I rummaged through the bushes. My former partner was lying in a heap between two holly trees, barely visible even when I was only inches away.

"Nolan?" I knelt beside her. "Are you okay?"

"Uggh."

"What happened?" I cradled her head.

She blinked several times. Rolled over onto her hands and knees and shook her head several times. "The doctor packs a mean right hook."

"She decked you?"

"Yep." Nolan stood up. "Must have taken off with the kid."

I started to say something but stopped when a shaft of light penetrated the shrubbery.

"Out here, where I can see you." Tom Maguire's voice was shaky yet forceful. He was on the house side of the line of shrubs, the alley a tantalizing though probably fatal escape route.

"Don't even think about it," he said.

"We're coming out," I said. "My partner is hurt."

Nolan and I stepped out of the bushes and into the glare from Maguire's flashlight.

"Where's Nazari?"

"She punched my lights out and then took off." Nolan rubbed her jaw.

No response. I imagined the wheels turning in his head, calculating and planning the next move. The suburban landscape was strangely still. No joggers, no people out walking dogs. I heard a worn-out muffler chug a few blocks away.

"Which way?" Maguire said.

"I was out cold," Nolan said. "Couldn't really see, now, could I?"

"What about you?" Maguire jiggled the light over my face.

"I was heading for the car, didn't see what happened either."

"How convenient." He pointed the muzzle of the Ruger at my knee-cap.

The chugging muffler grew closer.

"That's the police," Nolan said.

Tom Maguire cocked his head to one side, seemingly to position one ear for a better listen.

A rattling pickup rounded the corner. By the dim light of the street-lamp I could read the sign on the side. TOOGOODE AND TOOGOODE, CONTRACTORS.

The truck stopped a few feet from the alley.

"What the hell?" Maguire lowered the pistol until it was out of sight of whoever was in the pickup.

The truck turned and drove over the curb and onto Anita Nazari's yard. The headlights illuminated the three of us.

"That's not the police." Maguire swayed a little on his feet, and I re-alized Pendergast had inflicted a fair amount of damage on the man.

Because the headlights were shining on us, I couldn't see who was driving. Because the muffler was worn, the series of soft explosions was hard to discern against the rattling of the truck's motor.

What wasn't hard to hear or see was Tom Maguire yelping and dropping the gun and flashlight on the lawn. The rat-a-tat pops kept coming, sounding like tiny spits of anger in the still night air.

Tom screamed once and fell over on his back.

He looked like a pincushion, his body studded with large-gauge nails.

"Get in," Petey's soft voice called from the truck.

I shoved Nolan toward the passenger side and we climbed in.

CHAPTER FIFTY-ONE

Petey drove us to a piece of land a few miles away from Anita Nazari's house, on the far edges of the northern expansion of the vast sea of humans that was Dallas. He stopped in a clearing by a creek and a line of post oak trees growing along a barbed-wire fence.

A new Winnebago was parked there, as were two smaller travel trailers. Colleen came out and greeted us, smiling this time. Bria and her daughter were there, too, but the old woman was not.

Petey had told us they'd left the Travelers and were going out on their own. He smiled and pointed at the trailers. "Ain't they beauts?"

I introduced Nolan to everybody and then said, "Ever considered getting an apartment somewhere?"

Petey laughed and shook his head. "Ya still don't get our ways, do you?"

Colleen served us a meal on a portable picnic table set up by the tree line. By the soft glow of Coleman gas lamps, we ate brisket and beans under a canopy of Texas stars, washing down the food with pink wine.

Petey wouldn't say how he'd come to be in the area at exactly the right time. He mentioned something about wanting to see where his cousin had died. Then he told us the nail gun used to dispatch Tom Maguire had belonged to Collin Toogoode.

"Maybe Collin's spirit told me where to be." He winked at me. "What's the word . . . ironic . . . that his tool dispatched his killer."

I didn't have the heart to tell him that the killer of his cousins had probably died in the house a few minutes before. What was the point? I nodded and drank some more wine.

When it was time for bed, Colleen directed Nolan and me to one of the other trailers. We had it to ourselves and in a few minutes collapsed in the side–by-side twin beds in exhaustion.

The next morning, at Nolan's request, Petey drove us to the nearest Cadillac dealership, a sprawling place in McKinney, where we entered the showroom and were met with stares.

I must admit, we both looked like a year's worth of bad Saturday nights rolled into one, dirty and disheveled with clothes that were torn and smelly.

Nolan got pissy when no one would wait on us. She made a series of phone calls, and sixty minutes later we were headed south on U.S. Highway 75 toward Dallas in a brand-new Escalade. She had me drive while she called a real estate agent and made arrangements to list for sale the house she and Rufus had shared.

As the skyline of Big D slowly materialized in front of us, she said, "It's good to be rich."

I nodded but didn't say anything.

Forty minutes later I dropped her off at the house, right as the Realtor pulled up. I drove to the Target on Central Expressway in the shadow of downtown and bought several sets of clothes and a pay-as-you-go cell phone. I had about four hundred dollars in cash left. More was in the bank, but until I learned what was going on, I was reluctant to leave a paper trail.

I checked into a budget motel a few blocks away, not trusting my former accommodations for the time being. The guy behind the front desk owed me a favor from an incident involving his younger brother and a thug named Stumpy. He let me pay for three nights in cash and wrote down a fake name and address in the register.

I went to my room, showered, and dressed in fresh clothes, Levi 505s, a black T-shirt, and black Nikes.

By the time I was ready to hit the streets, it was noon and my stomach was rumbling. I headed east on Henderson Avenue in the new Escalade, into the heart of old East Dallas, my home for a number of years.

I stopped when I found a Mexican-food restaurant where the parking lot was full of trucks with lawn and construction equipment in the back.

I sat at a booth in the back, the only gringo in the place. Over a plate of enchiladas and tacos, I made several calls from the new cell, discreet inquiries into the events that had occurred the previous evening at Anita Nazari's home.

Three bodies had been found, each wearing a suit. One outside near the shrubs by the alley, obviously the man who called himself Tom Maguire. Another inside, on the floor of the kitchen, the man known as John Jordan. The third was Jordan's backup guy, discovered in the bushes of a house several lots down.

No mention of a man in golf clothes.

I ate a taco and then drank some iced tea.

After paying the bill, I called Anita Nazari's office number from the parking lot of the restaurant. Her assistant answered and told me she had been in briefly that morning to sign some papers. Then she had left.

I ended the call and drove to the VA hospital.

CHAPTER FIFTY-TWO

My friend's room was empty. The bed lay waiting for its next occupant, the covers stretched tight and crisp across the thin mattress. I went to the nurses' station and asked an obese woman in purple scrubs what happened.

"Baxter? Mike Baxter?" She frowned and stroked her chin. "He passed a day or so ago, I think."

I leaned against the hospital wall and closed my eyes, a canyon suddenly appearing in the middle of my stomach, a deep sorrow for all the lives lost or damaged beyond repair because of a few barrels of oil or an unnamed hill somewhere.

"You okay?" The woman touched my arm.

"Yeah." I opened my eyes and blinked several times. "I'm fine."

"He was a friend of yours?"

I nodded.

"Sorry."

"Do you know exactly when he died?" I tried to remember when I had spoken with Susan, wondered if she'd had time to come and visit her father.

"I just came on day shift." The woman picked up a stack of files from the countertop. "You can ask my supervisor."

"He had a daughter," I said. "Do you know if she stopped by?"

The woman shook her head and began leafing through the medical charts.

I left that floor and wandered around the lobby until I found the chaplain's office tucked in a corner by a flower shop.

The rotund middle-aged woman wearing a priest collar and gold reading glasses looked up when I pushed open the frosted glass door.

"May I help you?" she said.

"I'm looking for information on a friend of mine." I let the door close behind me. "He died here a day or two ago. His name is . . . was Mike Baxter."

She picked up a file from the corner of her desk and flipped it open. After scanning the contents for a few moments, she put it back where it had been resting but didn't say anything.

"Do you know anything about him?" I said.

No reply.

"Would it help if I spelled his name?" I tried not to sound sarcastic.

"Indigent burial." She took off her glasses.

"What does that mean?"

"He put in the paperwork a few days ago, requesting assistance with his interment." She twirled the glasses around in one hand.

"Is there a service planned?"

She nodded. "Two o'clock. Today."

"Where?" I looked at my watch. It was one thirty now.

She frowned as if I should have been able to read her mind.

"Give me a hint." I sighed. "The VFW hall?"

"No. Try the Dallas–Fort Worth National Cemetery." She pulled a postcard from a desk drawer and slid it across the desk.

Once back in the Escalade, I looked at the card and tried to figure out the fastest route to the cemetery. Dallas was my home, her streets the arteries that fed my livelihood. I knew every inch of the city, or so I thought until I looked at the address. Mountain Creek Parkway meant nothing to me. Mountains and Dallas in the same breath was an oxymoron.

I entered the address into the dash-mounted GPS and a few seconds later saw the location of the facility, in the far southwest corner of the county, by a large lake. The southern half of Dallas peeled by my windscreen as I weaved in and out of traffic on Illinois Avenue, past several new subdivisions and shopping centers with all the signs in Spanish.

Illinois Avenue and most signs of civilization ended abruptly at the Walton Walker Freeway, where the road I'd been on changed names to Mountain Creek.

I wouldn't go so far as to call them mountains, more like very large hills, but the terrain might as well have been from the moon for all the resemblance it bore to most of the flat North Texas landscape. The road became narrow and bumpy, nothing visible on either side due to the thick vegetation.

After a few hundred yards, the thick mass of trees and shrubs petered out and the lake became visible, a power plant the size of a stadium belching steam on one shore. The entrance to the cemetery appeared on my left, a simple yet elegant stone wall bearing the name of the place, surrounded by a carpet of green, carefully manicured grass.

I didn't know what to expect, but the lump of emotion that lodged in my throat upon seeing row after row of perfectly arranged gray headstones took me by surprise. The cemetery had only been open for a few years, but already it seemed full. I drove on and finally saw empty green spaces as I passed an administration building on the right.

In the distance, near a small lake surrounded by gravestones, were three cars and a group of people. I drove that way and parked behind the Toyota Prius with a FREE TIBET sticker on the bumper that had been in front of Susan Baxter's place.

I got out and stood beside the Escalade as two workmen lowered the pine coffin into the ground and the mourners headed my way.

Five people total. Olson. A priest. A middle-aged sergeant in full dress uniform. An elderly woman using a walker to get around. And Susan, wearing a black skirt and white top.

Olson whistled once as he looked at the gleaming new Cadillac. "Nice ride."

"It's not mine. Belongs to Nolan."

"How is the new widow holding up these days?"

"I think I resent your implications."

"I think I don't care." He looked once at Susan Baxter, who was walking toward me. "Where have you been the last few days?"

"Leave me alone." I crossed my arms.

My friend shrugged once and got into his car.

Susan walked to where I stood. Her eyes were red-rimmed.

"I'm sorry," I said.

"He told me he loved me."

I nodded.

"Said he was sorry for the way things happened."

"He was a good man."

"I just don't understand why." She rubbed her nose with the back of one hand.

"Why what?"

"Why anything?" She shook her head and got in the Prius.

The gravediggers filled in the hole. After they finished, I walked up and down the rows of tombstones as thunderclouds formed overhead and the wind shifted, bringing with it the smell of lake water and ozone.

After a while I got back in the Cadillac and drove north to the Time Out Tavern, a few blocks from Max's place. I nodded hello to the day drinkers and sat at the bar, nursing a Shiner Bock for an hour until I switched to scotch. I wasn't sure what happened after that.

CHAPTER FIFTY-THREE

Anita Nazari took a sip of latte and watched the people wander down Broxton Avenue in the Westwood section of Los Angeles. She and Mira were sitting outside at a coffee shop on the corner of Weyburn and Broxton. A palm tree jutted skyward from a grated hole in the sidewalk, the fronds dappling sunlight across their table.

Anita assumed most of the pedestrians were students at nearby UCLA, where she had just accepted a position as temporary professor at the David Geffen School of Medicine.

The women dressed so differently than in her college days: short denim skirts; tight, belly-baring tops. The men wore cargo shorts and sandals and colorful T-shirts featuring cleverly obscure slogans.

Broxton was a tree-lined avenue, two- and three-story buildings on either side of the street offering a myriad of collegiate goods: clothing, books, electronics, incense, and inexpensive food. The pedestrians outnumbered the cars, unique for most parts of Southern California, giving the area an almost East Coast feel.

"Do you like our new house?" Mira put down the book she'd been reading, one of the Lemony Snicket series, just purchased from a mystery bookstore down the street.

"Yes, darling." Anita patted her hand. "What about you?"

"I wish it had a pool."

"Maybe in our next place." Anita looked at the folder containing a six-month lease for a bungalow on Tavistock Avenue, on the west side of the campus. The rate was exorbitant, but the house had been recently updated and was in a desirable area near the 405. That, combined with her request for a short rental term, ensured she would be spending top dollar.

"Are we gonna move again real soon?" Mira asked.

"I don't know, darling. I wish I did."

Mira picked up her book but didn't open it.

"After lunch, let's go see your new school and get you enrolled," Anita said. "I'm sure you'll make many friends there."

"I miss my friends in Texas." Mira's voice sounded wistful.

"We'll be very happy here." Anita smiled. "I just know it."

Mira nodded and opened the book. Neither mother nor daughter spoke for a while. The parade of people walking down the sidewalk continued. A young man with a shaved head and wearing a red T-shirt sat down at the table next to them and opened an Apple laptop.

As Anita finished her coffee, Mira spoke again. "He looked like the building inspector."

"What?" Anita stared at her daughter.

"One of the men in the kitchen that night, when I came downstairs." Mira snapped her book shut. "He looked like the inspector I saw in the alley."

"I thought we agreed never to talk about that again." Anita wondered for the thousandth time where her ex-husband was. How he had survived. The Plano police department had been all too eager to write off what had occurred as the result of a botched home invasion, with no explanation whatsoever about the official status of the man claiming to be an FBI agent, found dead on the premises.

"I don't remember agreeing," Mira said. "I mostly remember you telling me we weren't gonna talk about it again."

"And when exactly did you see this man?" Anita felt a chill as she realized how close her former spouse had been without her knowing.

"The day before, I think." Mira looked at the ground. "I'm tired of things we're not supposed to talk about."

"Someday when you're older, you'll understand."

Mira crossed her arms. "And tired of moving all the time."

"I-I-I'm sorry." Anita felt the tears well in her eyes as she leaned across the table and kissed her daughter's forehead. She'd tried so hard to give her child a life different than her own—and had failed. "I wish I could explain."

"I wish you could, too."

"Let's go, then, okay?" Anita stood.

"I have to go to the bathroom first."

Anita nodded, and together they walked inside the coffee shop.

They were halfway down Broxton, near the parking garage where Anita had left the rental car, when Mira stopped as if she'd run into a wall.

"My new book," she said.

"Please don't tell me you've already lost it."

"I left it at the coffee place." Mira turned around and ran back toward Weyward, dodging people on the sidewalk.

"Wait for me." Anita followed as fast as possible.

Mira disappeared from view for a moment. Anita felt the fear rise from the pit of her stomach as she frantically scanned the sea of bodies on the sidewalk.

The crowd shifted.

Anita dodged between two women carrying oversized knapsacks. At the corner, she saw Mira stopped for the crosswalk sign.

"Please, don't run away again like that." Anita placed a hand on her daughter's shoulder and tried to control her panicked breathing.

"My book, Mama." Mira looked up and smiled. "I just want to get my new Lemony Snicket. It's a good one."

The light changed.

Mira and Anita walked hand in hand across the street.

At the store, the table was as they left it, an empty coffee cup next to Mira's plastic juice bottle. Between the two sat Mira's book. The table next to theirs, where the young man had been, was empty.

Anita gasped as she approached.

"Look, Mama." Mira picked up a pair of mirrored sunglasses from her book. "These are just like the kind the building inspector had."

CHAPTER FIFTY-FOUR

Seven days after Mike's funeral, with no threats or rumblings on the street, I gathered my meager possessions from the extended-stay hotel by Love Field and moved into the servants' quarters of Nolan's new home, a smaller but no less expensively furnished place than the one she'd shared with her husband.

It was only for a month or two, we both told ourselves. Only until I figured out a plan for my life.

Seven days after that, I was drinking coffee on the patio of a bookstore in the Uptown section of Dallas, an area of high-rise apartments and trendy restaurants. I was watching a table full of twenty-something women talk to each other. Their conversation centered on the latest fashions, which, judging by their outfits, were all about very short skirts.

I was smiling to myself and leafing through the latest issue of *Guns and Ammo* when a man in a fake beard and trench coat sat down at my table.

The temperature was in the eighties, and his cheeks and forehead glistened with sweat. Several of the women at the next table pointed and spoke to each other, covering their mouths with their hands.

He licked his lips repeatedly and looked from side to side, obviously trying to be surreptitious.

"You auditioning for the CIA or what?" I said.

He pulled his coat tighter.

"You're also blocking the view." I nodded toward the table where a couple of the women were now laughing.

"I'm a friend of Max's," he said.

"Dead Max?"

He nodded.

"What's your name, Friend of Dead Max?"

"That's unimportant."

"Okay, what do I call you?"

"You don't." He leaned forward, his hands on the table. "You just listen."

"We do this my way or not at all." I placed my right hand on top of his and squeezed, getting his index finger in a very uncomfortable position.

"Owww. That hurts." The man's voice was nasally, almost childlike.

"Why are you here?" I maintained pressure.

"To warn you." He squirmed in his seat. "Jeez, I'm trying to help."

I let go of his hand as the group of women got up and left.

"You hired Max to track down someone, right?" Trench Coat said.

I nodded. "Collin Toogoode."

"Shh." The man looked around the coffee shop. "They are everywhere."

"No, they're not." I drained my coffee. "If they were, I'd be dead by now."

"He's not what tipped them off anyway."

I raised an eyebrow.

"It was the woman's name."

"Anita Nazari?" I kept my voice low, remembering now that as we were leaving his apartment, Nolan had asked Max to check up on her, too.

"Right." He nodded slowly. "We ran her through a couple of databases we shouldn't have. Her name rang all kinds of bells."

"She was being threatened by a man named Pendergast."

"That would be one of those names you don't want to say out loud ever again."

"Who did Pend . . . he work for?"

"Nearest I can tell, he was freelancing for a small firm owned by a multinational drug company." The man paused and looked around before continuing. "A competitor of Fortunary."

"And that means what?"

The man sighed. "Fortunary manufactured the antibiotics given to a lot of the soldiers during the Gulf War. Supposed to be harmless."

"But Nazari proved they weren't."

He shook his head. "The doctor whose name we shouldn't be saying either proved that they *maybe* weren't harmless. Nothing definitive."

"That's it?" I said. "All these people died because of a maybe?"

"Do you know what Fortunary's market cap is? How much money vanishes if the shares slide a few dollars?"

"A few pieces of silver." I shook my head. "So he wanted her to keep going with the research, right?"

"Bingo." The man nodded. "Fortunary put Tom Maguire into place to keep an eye on her. Track her experiments. The other company, the competitor of Fortunary, learned about it and hired someone to take Maguire out. But for some reason he didn't."

"Pendergast," I said softly. "He let Maguire live because eliminating him would alert the other side."

"You think?" The man adjusted his fake beard. "Friends close and enemies closer, I guess."

"Or because he wouldn't get the chance to do the bunny-boiling routine for his wife. Hell if I know anything anymore." I rubbed the bridge of my nose, tired even though it was only midmorning. Anita Nazari had been a brutally frustrating individual, at times sweet and caring, other times condescending and manipulating in the extreme. I'd spent maybe three days total with her, and I wanted to break her neck. I could only imagine being married to that.

"Enough with that name already," Trench Coat said.

I ignored his comment. "But Maguire and the FBI were working on the same side, right?"

"Why am I talking to stupid people?" The man looked skyward as if addressing a celestial being.

"Jordan was FBI. He and Maguire were on the same team."

The man laughed. "You really think this Jordan dude was getting a paycheck drawn on the U.S. Treasury?"

"He had a full FBI assault team."

The man shook his head and smiled. "Let's just say it's hard to tell where corporate America ends and the government begins."

"Why did you track me down and tell me this?"

"I thought you should know." He craned his neck, looking from side to side. "They're bound to come after you."

"Because if they let me live I might tell somebody?" I stood and tossed my coffee cup away.

"Finally you're getting it." He got up, too. "I was worried you might be, like, stupid or something."

"And I'll prove it with what?"

He stared at me for a moment before walking away.

I debated getting another cup of coffee. I thought about calling Nolan to see if she wanted to go shoot pool somewhere.

One of the women who had been sitting nearby came back. She picked up a folder that had been left on the table and smiled at me.

I smiled back, walked over, and said, "Hello."

"Hi." She ran one hand through her blond hair like an oversize brush. No wedding ring. "I see you in here a lot."

"Nice place to watch the world go by." I introduced myself. She did the same, and we shook hands.

"You work around here?" She tucked the folder under one arm.

I nodded but didn't say anything. I had been ready for anything but that.

"I just got this new job. Been in training all week." She raised her eyebrows in mock exasperation. "We had a huge test this morning."

"Where do you work?" I motioned to a chair. She sat down, and I followed suit.

"I'll office out of my apartment." She crossed her legs and leaned back. "I'm going to be a pharmaceutical rep."

"Really?" I nodded and pursed my lips. "I had a friend who used to work for Fortunary."

"Oh, the job's not with them." She shook her head and mentioned the name of a corporation I had never heard of. "Fortunary's not hiring right now."

I looked at my watch. "Want to grab an early lunch?"

"Sure." She smiled shyly.

We both stood at the same time and headed for the gate in the waist-high patio fence.

"So what happened to your friend?" She stepped through the opening and onto the sidewalk running alongside McKinney Avenue.

"He died suddenly, not long ago." I headed south, walking on the street side. "Had a chemical problem. You know how it goes."